PROPELLERHEAD

By

Ron Martelet

4th Edition

Anecdotes from a lifetime love affair with aviation

©Copyright 2006 - 2008

Ron Martelet

A propellerhead is someone who is interested in all aspects of aviation.

Someone who eats, drinks and sleeps airplanes.

Acknowledgements

I wish to thank both Dave Luther and Rick Hance for their help on this book. Without them it would never have been published.

Contents

MY AUNT BEANIE 1

MODEL AIRPLANES 3

THE BEGINNING 5

AIRPORT 6

GLIDER/SAILPLANE 14

WOMEN OF ADVENTURE 15

WHAT DID YOU HAVE FOR LUNCH? 18

BIG JOHN 21

NO TWO ARE ALIKE 22

NATURAL BORN PILOT: 22

HIGH TIME PILOT: 23

GRANDMA: 23

BORED: 25

DOING TWO THINGS AT THE SAME TIME 26

MOTORCYCLE MAMA 27

BIG MAMA 28

I DON'T FEEL SMALL BUT I GUESS I AM 29

HOW MUCH WOULD YOU PAY TO GET SICK 31

MY HERO 33

WOMEN SAY THE DARNDEST THINGS 34

WAS IT GOOD FOR YOU?	35
DRUNKS	36
SWEET SIXTEEN WITH A BROKEN HEART	39
THE NATURAL	40
AIRLINE PILOTS	42
THE DAY WE CLOSED RTE 30	44
I AM A NICE GUY	48
TEST PILOT	50
UNDUE CONCERN	51
NEVER TRUST A TOW PILOT WEARING A CRASH HELMET	53
EVERYBODY WANTS TO GO TO HEAVEN BUT NOBODY WANTS TO DIE	55
FEAR	59
THREE STAGES	61
STICK TIME	62
"HI SAILOR, WANT TO GO FOR A RIDE"?	64
BUYING A SHARE	66
THE CESSPOOL 150/150	69
DUTCH	71
THE "P" FACTOR	73
DORT	75

WILBUR	78
SPIN OFFS	85
LIFT IS WHERE YOU FIND IT	87
STINKY DOG	92
BROWN EYES	95
GOOD IN VEGETABLE SOUP	97
A REAL AIRPLANE	99
THE DAY WE BURIED BILL	100
BE CONSIDERATE OF OTHER PEOPLE	105
DROP IN ANYTIME	106
OUTLANDINGS	110
BEAUTY IS IN THE EYE OF THE BEHOLDER	113
THE PITH BALL VARIOMETER	115
BUILDING YOUR OWN	121
SHOPPING	124
IT WAS GOOD ENOUGH FOR THE LUFTWAFFE	127
RUDDER FLUTTER	130
THE MANAGER	133
NAMING YOUR SHIP	135
PARACHUTE	137
BIG BONED WOMAN	139
I CALLS UM LIKE I SEES UM	141

AIRIAL SURVEILLANCE	142
OH, TO HEAR THE COWS MOO!	144
LOST PROPELLER	147
FAMILIARITY BREEDS CONTEMPT	150
TOAST	152
WINTER FLIGHT	154
HIGHSCHOOL CLASS	157
THE LAST HURRAH	159
APPARITION	163
SHIT HAPPENS	165
MY FAVORITES	168
MIKE	173
TRANSITION PILOTS	175
MOLLY AND THE MONI	177
CLOUDS	178
FOUR BOX TOPS AND A DIME	181
BOOMER	183
THE END	186
ABOUT THE AUTHOR	187

MY AUNT BEANIE

Aunt "Beanie" was the one with the cookie jar. I wish I had a dollar for every time I got caught with my hand in that jar. "Beanie" was not her name of course, it was Bernice. As a small child, "Beanie" was what came out of my mouth when I tried to say Bernice. It stuck and from then on she was "Beanie" to everyone. She was the one who revealed to me that I was a propellerhead long before I could remember.

One day when I was in the Navy I visited Aunt Beanie while on leave. She said she had something she wanted to show me. She opened a door and on the back was something I had never seen before. It was two small pieces of wood nailed together. One piece was shorter than the other one and it was nailed over the longer one at a right angle, closer to one end than the other. The nails were too long; they stuck out and were bent over.

After looking at the thing awhile I commented that I must have been a very religious child to have made her a crucifix. Aunt Beanie said, "That is no cross, that is your first airplane". I wonder how old I was when I built that thing? I must have been a propellerhead even before I could remember.

Aunt Beanie is long gone now. As a child I loved her cookies, as an adult I loved her. Everyone should have an aunt like my Aunt "Beanie".

My First Airplane

MODEL AIRPLANES

Model airplanes changed my life. I really do believe that and this is why.

You might say that school didn't come easy to me, in fact you might say I had a hell of a time of it at first. It took me five years to get through the first three grades. There were a number of reasons for my not doing well at first. For one thing, I started a little young. I had all the childhood diseases a kid could have in the first year of school. I had two younger sisters at home and I couldn't understand why they could stay at home while I had to go to school.

In the third grade I ran into a Nun who had taken her vows in Buchenwald. Her name was Sister Mary Cruelty. She failed half the class and I was in that half. Still the biggest reason I didn't do well in school was that I didn't like school. Anyhow by the time I got out of the third grade I had a real lock on the job of village idiot.

They say every cloud has a silver lining. During the brief period between my Korean War service and my college education I applied for many jobs. When I came to the part on the job application where it asked me to circle how many years of education I had completed, it gave me great pleasure to circle "14"; and everybody thought I had two years of college.

It must have been during the summer vacation between the third and fourth grades when out of sheer boredom I wandered into the public library. It was there that I discovered an old dusty box of model aviation magazines. I began to leaf through them and really became interested in what the pages revealed. Then I realized that I couldn't read all the words on the pages and I wanted to. All of a sudden I had a reason to learn to read. Some of the pages had plans for the planes that were pictured there and they had dimensions on them. Now I had a reason to learn numbers and math.

So I became interested in model airplanes. I bought a kit and tried to build it. At first I wasn't very successful but I was stubborn and kept trying. I finally got one built but couldn't get the thing to fly. This opened a whole new field of knowledge for me, Aerodynamics. Soon I was learning all about center of gravity, thrust line, dihedral, angle of incidence and on and on.

I began getting better grades in school because now I had a reason to learn all the stuff that I didn't care about learning before. By the time I was in the eighth grade I was a good student and by the time I was in high school I was getting "A"s and "B"s, in the courses I liked, of course.

I wonder how many people could tell the same story? I think most kids that are not doing well in school just need to find something that sparks their interest.

I became quite good at building models and began to fly them in competition and this opened up the need for even more knowledge. It became necessary to study design, drafting, structures, etc, etc.
Model aviation is a hobby that has stuck with me all my life. I still build and fly a model now and then when I am not working on building or flying a full size plane.

Someone once said to me, "Building a full size plane sure must beat messing around with models". Not true, models are every bit as much fun as real planes, at least I think so. If it were not for models perhaps I would not be building big ones today.

I wonder where I would be today if I hadn't discovered that old dusty box of model airplane magazines?

THE BEGINNING

It was on the return flight from a late season ski trip in Colorado. My skiing buddy in the seat next to me asked a question that would change my life forever. "What are you going to do this summer Ron?" I told him I was going to sail my boat as usual, as I had done for the past nine years. He then told me he was going to learn to fly a glider. I was somewhat surprised, as I didn't know you could do that in Illinois. I thought you had to live in California or Arizona or some place like that with mountains. I thought that might be fun so I told him I might join him.

On a bright spring day in 1973 I showed up at Hinckley Soaring, a glider field 60 miles west of Chicago, to take a ride and see what it was all about. That was the beginning. I was hooked from the very first flight and signed up for the private pilot glider course before I left the field that day.

I believe soaring appeals to people who like to ski and sail. All three sports don't require an engine and rely on a certain amount of skill to get from one spot to another. People who prefer powered flight seem to also prefer snowmobiles and powerboats.

AIRPORT

Trailer Office

"Bye honey, I'm going to the airport," I call as I head out the door. The airport, Hinckley Airport, my airport, is three miles west of my back door. It used to be 50 miles from my back door. When I retired I fixed that; I bought a two-and-a-half car garage with an attached house in the town of Hinckley, Illinois. My latest homebuilt project, a Kolb Firestar II occupies half of the garage, when it isn't occupying the entire garage. I hope to get it completed before I go to the nursing home. My Mitchell B10 ultralight sits in a trailer behind the garage. It is ten-years old now, and of all the things I fly, I love it the best.

Most small airports are somewhat similar, and yet each one has its own character. Hinckley Airport has lots of character. Twenty-six hundred feet of east/west sod runway, sits back north about 150 yards from Illinois Route 30. An "s" turn gravel drive goes to the small parking area.

Except in years of severe drought, there is always a big puddle of water at the first part of the "s"-turn. At first, I thought there was some sort of spring there. No matter how many loads of large size gravel are dumped on the puddle it keeps re-appearing. Perhaps there is some sort of geological phenomenon occurring. The earth in that particular spot, absorbs gravel, converts it to water and pumps it back to the surface to form a puddle. Anyhow, if you wash your car, drive to the airport and then drive it home, you will have to wash your car again.

The office is a gutted- out mobile home that sits adjacent to the northeast corner of the parking area. A small raised wooden deck was built on the north side of the trailer complete with a railing, built-in benches and a fiberglass roof.

The ground skirt around the trailer is loose in places, which provides access for skunks, cats, raccoons and God knows to what else. If you should be so unfortunate as to drop something on the deck, and it goes through the cracks, you had best let it be.

The benches provide a shaded resting place for tired glider pilots just returned from their unending search for the ever-elusive thermals, power pilots who have been told soaring is cheaper than powered flight, and civilians who want to know if the glider will crash if the wind quits.

Other types to be occasionally found there are the sweet young thing in short shorts and halter top, which proves to be very disruptive to the entire operation. Tow pilots, who normally run over each other to take the next tow, seem to no longer care. Tow planes sit empty, their doors agape. Line boys walk past the porch again and again, casting sidelong glances. All the while, six gliders sit at the end of the field waiting to get airborn.

Then there is the distraught mother, yelling at her young son who is jumping off the porch railing with out-stretched arms trying to fly, and at her daughter who has just spilled grape soda on her white dress. Later that day I saw the kid after she had spilled more pop on herself, this time it was cherry. She looked like she was dressed for a "Grateful Dead" concert.

In the front of the trailer sit a couple of picnic tables which are occasionally actually used for picnics. Most of the time, though, they are occupied by pilots, instructors and students, all of them describing some sort of aerial maneuver with their hands zooming back and forth in the air. If a Martian were to land and observe this, it would report back to Mars that Earthlings converse mainly with their hands. Often times one of these pilots will have forgotten the cheeseburger on the gas grill, which will be emitting copious amounts of black smoke. When finally retrieved, the Martian would likely observe that Earthlings eat small asteroids covered with molten lava.

As you enter the trailer you will see that the West End has a small space, about 8X10 feet, separated from the rest of the trailer by a glass case. There is a desk, chair, telephone, radio, file cabinet, cash register and about 10 people in that space. This is the heart of the operation, the command center, sort of, like you see on TV, when they launch the space shuttle, sort of.

It is here that calls are taken from the far-flung corners of the earth. People call to schedule a glider ride for their grandmother. They ask pertinent questions like, "Will a pilot go up with her or will she go up alone?" and of course my favorite," Will the glider crash if the wind quits?" Glider rentals and student lessons are booked. Weather reports and forecasts are given, usually optimistically. Any wind that doesn't rip the roof off the trailer is referred to as light and variable. Ceilings and visibility are treated similarly.

It is here that bills are written up, cash is received, change is made, merchandise is sold, and the key to the wash room is kept.

The aforementioned glass case holds some interesting stuff and a few things that aren't interesting at all. There is a smattering of dusty instruments, wing tip wheels, tow hooks and some other glider parts. Training manuals, owner's manuals, F.A.R.s and test standards are neatly stacked there along with a goodly supply of sick sacks. T-shirts, hats and sunglasses are also on display.

Next to this case is a magazine rack, which holds aviation publications, some rather old and some current, all of them well thumbed. A line of fiberglass and steel chairs are along the north wall from the magazine rack to the door. Across from these chairs there is a refrigerator, chuck full of different flavored sodas. The door of the refrigerator is lined with shelves, which contain remnants of lunches, some of which have turned various shades of blue and green. A microwave oven sits on a small table next to the refrigerator. I have never seen anyone use it. People seem to prefer to incinerate their food on the gas grill.

In the southeast corner of the "Great Room," shall we call it, sits the exploding gas furnace. In the early spring and late fall, a contest goes on to see who can cajole whom into lighting this beast off. The trick is to get the pilot lit. This usually takes at least seven tries. Once the pilot is lit, the main valve is turned on and the blower switch is flicked on. Now all those in the know stand around in a semi-circle and stare at the beast. With a great "whoosh" and a bang the main jet lights off and the furnace door leaves its moorings and flies half way across the room falling with a terrible clatter to the floor. Someone always picks it up and puts it back on its hinges, knowing full well that the next time it lights off the same thing will happen all over again. This is great fun for all the old timers but I have seen new students log considerable flight time when this occurs.

One cold late fall evening, I decided to sleep on the floor of this trailer. We won't go into the events that led up to this decision, but let me say it wasn't one of my better ones. Between the furnace blowing up every hour on the hour, the 18 wheelers rolling by on route 30, the freight trains on the tracks next to the highway and the mice scurrying around, I didn't get a whole heck of a lot of sleep.

The Japanese have a saying, "As noisy as a mouse," just the opposite of what we say here in the USA. If you ever heard a mouse dragging a candy bar wrapper around at 2 a.m., you would agree with the Japanese.

There is a table and four more chairs sitting next to the exploding furnace. For some reason the tabletop always has a sticky coating of soda pop. On a hot summer day, a logbook can become pretty firmly attached to the tabletop. Great care must be taken to dislodge it or it will tear. No matter how often it gets scrubbed, it just always seems to be sticky. Many a happy hour has been spent sitting around that table discussing things aeronautical, and sometimes things not so aeronautical. The chair next to the furnace is the warmest but it is also the most dangerous. I wish I had a dollar for every time that furnace door hit me on the elbow.

On the East wall, right next to the table, is a black board that isn't black at all, it's green. There is always a chalk sketch on it, maybe some airfoil sections or remnants of where some instructor was drawing the landing pattern or glide slope on final. Occasionally there is a timely message like: "No negative G maneuvers with Passengers!" Forget that one and the supply of sick sacks goes down quickly.

The next little space behind that wall is only about five feet wide. It's our supply room. You'll find anything there, from lawn care products to aircraft engine oil. Tires, tubes, tow ropes and toilet paper, buckets, bolts and baling wire, it's all there, somewhere. Every spring, this place is put in beautiful order; everything is grouped neatly on the shelves. Half way through the season it looks like some giant got in there with a big stick and stirred it up. It's just another mystery like the puddle in the driveway or the sticky tabletop. There are a lot of mysteries like that in life.

The next and last room on the East End of the trailer has a character all its own. I like to think of it as our "Behavior Modification and Testing Laboratory". The accommodations are rather sparse, a table with one chair on each side. There is some other stuff piled in there, but one hardly notices it. A student sits on one side of the table, and the instructor (or a man from the F.A.A.) sits on the other side. Voices are always subdued back there.

I don't think I've ever heard anyone laugh in that room. Well, maybe a little nervous one now and then. Students enter there and some sweat on the coldest day. Students can be anyone, a boy 14 who can't drive a car legally or a man 55 who drives a 747 between Chicago and Los Angeles.

Now to go outside. Along the south side of the runway, from the trailer down to the east end the company ships are tied down. A couple of SGS 2-33A basic trainers are there in fresh new paint jobs. They remind me of elderly ladies in bright new dresses. What will we do when they are gone? In my estimation there is nothing being built that can replace them. There are other ships there too. The Grob 103, SGS 1-26, SGS 1-36, and last but not least the queen of the fleet, the Pegasus 102. What a joy it is to fly her. Pity, I haven't done that much. Seems I hang out with the elderly ladies mostly. Some wag is sure to say that's because I am an elderly man. Well, maybe so, but you can't do demos or instruction in a Pegasus 102.

Just west of the trailer and set back away is the hangar. During the winter it is full of disassembled tow planes and gliders. Somehow, every winter, room is made to refurbish the ships for the next season. Certain things stick in my mind. One early spring day, I stood alone in that hangar. It was cool and damp and still. An eerie light filtered through the big fiberglass door, and the smell of airplanes was all around me. The breeze outside rattled a handful of dry leaves along the bottom edge of the door. Then I heard an engine sputter to life somewhere. I heard the roar of the tow plane go by followed shortly by the swish of the glider. It was the first flight of the season. I will always remember that as though it was yesterday.

From the hangar west along the south edge of the runway there is more stuff. First comes a rather odd assortment of powered aircraft in various stages of disarray. There is one with no wings, then one with one wing but no engine, then one which seemingly has all its parts. As I recall, the last time I saw any of these fly, I had a lot more hair.

Next comes a row of long thin trailers. This is what I refer to as, "Big Guy Country." This is where the privately owned gliders are kept. These ships cost big bucks. I rarely venture into this territory, I feel out of place there, sort of like the greens keeper wandering into the dining room at the Country Club. The straw hat on my head and the towline safety link tied about my waist are a dead give away. Oh, they are nice enough guys. I know some of them personally, and they always speak to me, Still, I don't spend much time there. I'm afraid someone will call me "boy" and put me to work.

After the long thin trailers, there is an area that belongs to the jump operation, This is composed of a trailer, a big tent, a port-a-potty, a fire pit, a gutted out Beech D-18 fuselage, two operational Beech D-18's, a Cessna 180, and lots of young crazy people. Some not so young at that, I like these people, they add a lot to the atmosphere of the place on weekends. Screaming, hollering bodies suspended below brightly-colored chutes drift gently to earth.

Weekends at this airport are a regular airshow. The glider operation is in full swing, and everything from the 2-33A trainers to the latest and greatest high performance sailplane is taking off and landing. The Beech D18 goes thundering by with a load of jumpers, smiling and waving. The sound of those big radial engines almost knocks the breath out of you. It no sooner departs than the previous load of jumpers arrives, whooping and hollering under fluttering chutes.

We have our share of weekend airport hoppers, mostly Cessna 150's and Piper Cherokees; some of them abort their landing and go around three or four times before they finally plant the thing. It does get busy here. Sometimes we get a few homebuilts to visit. One morning, at 2000 feet I looked down and saw two World War II fighter aircraft go sailing past. It was like a time warp.

Twenty-five years have gone by since my buddy and I came to this airport to take a glider ride, and I am still here. I've lost track of him. Some of the faces that were here on that first day are still around, but most of them are new. Many have come and gone, some I remember and some I don't.

The airport is still here. I realize nothing is forever, and someday this will probably be a shopping mall. I just hope it doesn't happen in my lifetime, I love this place.

As the sun sinks below the horizon, the Beech goes roaring by spouting blue flames from its exhaust stacks. One last twilight jump run. Line boys and pilots are tying down gliders for the night. Tow pilots top off their ships' tanks and push them into the hanger for the night.

The lights are now on in the trailer. Logbooks are being filled out, cash is being counted, books are being balanced, and flying stories are being told. First liar doesn't stand a chance.

I'm sitting outside on the picnic table, cigar in one hand, and a beer in the other. A big yellow moon has just risen over the corn, and the crickets are setting up a racket. God, I can't wait for tomorrow.

GLIDER/SAILPLANE

Soaring pilots often refer to their sailplanes as gliders. In this book I use the terms interchangeably, there is a big difference however.
A glider is an aircraft, which can not achieve an altitude greater than that at which it is launched. A sailplane on the other hand, can gain altitude above its launch altitude. In other words it is capable of soaring.

The common yardstick for soaring performance of a sailplane is its lift/drag ratio or glide ratio. In other words, how far it can glide horizontally for a given loss of altitude. If a sailplane has a glide ratio or L/D of 40/1, it will be capable of going 40 miles from an altitude of 1 mile.

A basic trainer such as the SGS 2-33A will have a L/D of 23/1 and some of the high performance ships are as high as 50/1 and getting higher all the time. I sometimes wonder what the optimum glide ratio will be and if we will ever reach it.

It is pretty amazing when you consider that if a person was strong enough to lift a sailplane and its pilot six feet off the ground, while standing in the end zone of a football field and then throw it, it would go the entire length of the field before it would touch the ground. That's pretty efficient. Like I say, they are getting better all the time.

Sailplanes with that kind of performance are things of aerodynamic beauty and they don't come cheap. A glider with that kind of performance will cost around $65,000 and then of course you must have a $10,000 trailer to haul it around in.

It is possible to get into soaring for a fraction of the cost of course and probably have just as much fun. If you must have the best then it will cost you.

WOMEN OF ADVENTURE

A Demo Pilot is someone who demonstrates an aircraft to someone else, in other words someone who takes another person for a ride. To be a demo pilot you must have a Commercial glider pilots license, and then you get paid for flying, but not much.

After several hundred demo flights I have formed some definite opinions about people who take glider rides. First of all you can't tell a book by its cover and you can't tell how a passenger will react to a ride by looking at them.

It has always amazed me that I can take some big strapping farm guy up and he will request that I don't do anything but fly straight and level because turns bother him. On the other hand I can take some little gal up and she wants to do some stunts. After I have done everything possible with the glider she asks me to fly it upside down.

So, I guess generally speaking I have come away with the idea that women are more adventuresome than men. Oh, I know there are exceptions to the rule, but they may be the ones that prove it.

In the late summer of 1991, I received a phone call from a young man who at one time worked as manager of Hinckley Soaring. I was working there at that time as a part time demo pilot/instructor. He had gotten married about a year ago and he and his wife moved to Kauai, Hawaii. He was working as manager for "Tradewinds Glider Tours" there on the island and needed some help for a couple of weeks.

It seems one of his pilots got mad at the owner and just up and quit cold. He needed a replacement right now until he could find someone else full-time. He outlined the deal and told me how much money I would be guaranteed and how much I could possibly make. He said I would not be there more than two weeks. At first I was reluctant to go, after all I had commitments. Then I got to thinking it over. How often does a guy get a chance to go to Hawaii to fly gliders and get paid for it too? I figured even if I went in the hole for $500 it would be worth it. I went.

The glider I was flying out there was a Schweizer SGS 2-32 which is a three place ship. It carries the pilot in front and two passengers in the back seat. The passengers had to be very skinny or very friendly and preferably both.

Schweizer 2-32

That back seat was about 26 inches wide as I recall it now. It was amazing how big some of the couples were that I stuffed back there. At times I thought I was going to have to have them strip and rub themselves with Vaseline.

On the instrument panel in front of me was a big spring clip with a sign over it. The sign read, "Tipping is not expected but is greatly appreciated." Of course the sign was quite readable from the back seat. The first thing I did every morning was to stick a little seed money in the spring clip. A twenty and a couple of tens would do nicely.

I would stuff a couple in the back seat and off we would go into the wild blue yonder. After giving them the standard tour for awhile I would sometimes hear the magic words from the back seat. It was always the lady who said them. "Ron, if you make this flight exciting there will be something extra in it for you." Hot dog! Hell for $50 I would crash the damn thing.

I would do a couple of wing overs and a loop or two and that would usually do the job. Although this was very lucrative it was also very hard on my ears. A woman sitting directly behind you screaming at the top of her lungs while under a Plexiglas canopy must be the loudest sound in the world. It was always the lady who asked though, the guy never said much at all.

WHAT DID YOU HAVE FOR LUNCH?

Every person seems to have a different degree of tolerance to motion sickness. There is no way you can tell by looking at them. Many flights are ended prematurely at the passengers' request.

Early in my career as a demo pilot I had a passenger say he was becoming sick on a flight. I frantically searched the glider for a sick sack but couldn't find one. I finally handed him my hat. There is nothing I won't do to keep someone from messing up my glider. Spending a hot summer day in a glider after someone became ill in it is not a very pleasant experience. No matter how good a job the lineboys do of cleaning up it still smells.

From that day on I made sure I had my own private supply of sick sacks. Whenever I took a commercial flight I took every sick sack in sight. I was king of the sick sacks, I had them stashed everywhere.

The office usually had a good supply of them on hand but not always. One day a lady informed me that she sometimes became motion sick. This was before the previous described event and I didn't have my own supply of bags yet.

I asked the sixteen-year-old kid managing the office that day to give the lady a sack. He rummaged around awhile and then handed her a clear plastic bag that he had used to transport a couple of slices of pizza for his lunch. The inside of the bag was coated with tomato sauce, lumps of cheese and a few pieces of pepperoni. The lady became ashen white and said, "My God! Has this been used?"
He was a big strapping fellow and he informed me that he did a lot of sailing on Lake Michigan in some really rough weather and never became ill. Why he told me this I don't know, perhaps it was on his mind. You can guess what happened. He was what we demo pilots refer to as a "two bagger." He filled the bag I carried in my pocket and another bag that luckily was in the ship too. He just couldn't

believe he did that. I never saw anyone take it so hard. I told him it sometimes happens to the best of us but there was nothing I could do to console him.

After I started carrying my own sick sack neatly folded up in my shirt pocket where I could get at it quickly, I fell into a very bad habit. The sack wasn't used all that frequently so I began to record my flights on it, the number, duration and the type, stuff like that.

Towards the end of a particularly busy day I had a young lady passenger use it. We landed and I helped her out of the ship. She hurriedly walked away carrying the sack with outstretched arm. Then I realized that there go my records. I ran after her, caught up to her and asked if I might have the bag back. I have seen some really strange looks from women before in my life but never one like this. I wonder what was racing through her mind? She probably thought I was the kinkiest person she had ever met.

She was cuter than a bugs ear, an Oriental gal in her late twenties. She was dressed very nicely and had a pleasant personality. I really wanted to please her. I thought I was doing a good job of it. She chattered away continually. "Oh! Look at cow, so very tiny." "There is train, so small, look like toy train," and on and on.

After awhile I said, "you are really enjoying this aren't you"? "No," she replied "I am very sick." I couldn't believe my ears. I handed her a sick sack and was as gentle as I could be getting the glider back down. The moment the wheel stopped rolling the canopy flew open and she jumped out and ran away. I was so disappointed.

The pilot has a great advantage over the passenger when it comes to motion sickness; they know what they are about to do next. The passenger is just along for the ride and is often surprised when the glider changes direction or attitude rapidly. I always ask the passenger what kind of ride they want. Do they just want to float around in gentle wide turns or do they want to do aerobatics? I try to make it a pleasant experience for all of them.

Over the years there are some things I have learned about being a demo pilot. Besides asking what kind of flight they want and then giving it to them there are other things. Never discuss airsickness before the flight, the power of suggestion can be a bad thing. Regardless what a passenger tells you always watch for the signs. Sweat running down the back of the neck, hiccuping, extreme quiet, no head movement, you can tell. Unlike a power plane which can fly straight and stay up, a glider must circle in the rising air like a hawk or other soaring birds. Some people don't mind this at all but others can't take much of it.

There is one thing though that gets just about everyone sick and that is negative "G"s. If you dive the glider to gain speed, pull up into a zoom and then push the stick forward at the top of the zoom, there is a moment of weightlessness. Negative "G"s. About three of those are all anyone can take. There are exceptions to every rule however and one young gal couldn't seem to get enough.

When we landed she told me she thought it was better than a roller coaster.

BIG JOHN

Big John was a German sailplane pilot who really loved to soar. He must have loved it, because he had a real problem, it made him sick.

John tried everything, patches, pills, the whole nine yards and still he got sick. He just wouldn't quit. He flew with the stick in one hand and a bag in the other.

I loved to hear him recount his last soaring adventure. His enthusiasm was boundless. He would describe a two-hour flight in minute detail. How high he was, how far he flew, how low he got, how he had to scratch for lift, how he made a last minute save, how the clouds looked, and on and on.

John moved away and I didn't see him for a long time. Then one day he walked onto the field again. It must have been at least three years since I had last seen him.

He had retired. He had a big motor-home with his glider in a trailer behind it. He was just bumming around the country, flying at soaring sites wherever he found them. He was having a ball.

We talked for about an hour and a half. He still had the same passion for soaring, you could see it in his eyes and hear it in his voice. I asked him if he still got sick when he flew? He said, "Yeah."

NO TWO ARE ALIKE

Being a demo pilot/flight instructor in gliders you get to meet a lot of different people as passengers and students. No two are alike. They come from all walks of life, all races, both sexes, all sexual persuasions, and every shape and size you can imagine. Here are a few.

NATURAL BORN PILOT:

He wasn't a young man, I'd say about sixty. He was the quiet type and didn't have much to say. We got off tow at two thousand feet and hit a thermal immediately. At four thousand I asked him if he wanted to fly and he said yes if I would explain what to do.

I gave him a brief explanation and demonstration of the controls and turned him loose telling him to fly straight and level heading towards those smoke stacks on the horizon. He did it perfectly. I demonstrated a turn and told him to do a 180 to the left. He did it perfectly. "Well, it's pretty apparent that you have done some flying before" I remarked. He said he had never touched the controls before today. For the next five minutes I left him fly the thing. We flew straight and level this direction and that and did all kinds of turns and he did every thing perfect. He even rolled out of the turns on heading. Again I questioned him about being a pilot and his answer remained the same, "No never." I still don't believe him.

After instructing for a number of years I have come to the conclusion that I could pick one hundred people at random off the street and I could teach ninety-nine of those people to fly. There would be one who would just never learn to do it. Of the others that did, there would be one or two that would be better pilots than I could ever hope to be. Perhaps these people may have had previous experience but it doesn't matter. It is a feeling that comes back to me through the stick and rudder pedals that tells me they are naturals and I am not. It is hard for me to admit that but I feel it is true.

HIGH TIME PILOT:

As we walk down the line towards the glider we have been assigned, he tells me of all the ratings he holds, all the planes he has flown and all the hours he has in his log books. By the time we reach the ship I have had a belly full.

As the tow plane pulls us through one thousand feet I ask him if he would like to fly the ship. Of course he accepts my invitation. For the next minute or so we are on a roller coaster ride. We are in every possible attitude but upside down. I tell him I've got it, take the controls and get the glider back in position behind the tow plane. Then I let him take the controls again. Off we go into the wild blue yonder, and I do mean wild. Once again we are off on an ariel excursion that defies description. I can just imagine the kind of language that is coming out of the tow pilots mouth. I take the control again and then ask, "How many hours did you say you have?" Silence. Before me sits a far meeker man than the one who walked beside me down the flight line just a few moments ago.

To the uninitiated the tow portion of the flight looks like a piece of cake. After all, the tow plane is doing all the work. The glider is being dragged up into the sky by a long rope and the glider pilot has nothing to do but look out the window at the pretty view. Wrong! The glider seems to have a mind of it's own on tow. It wants to go everywhere but where it should want to go.

Students seem to have more trouble with the tow than any other part of their training. The tow really is an easy thing to do but it is not so easy to learn. It is sort of like learning to ride a bicycle. Once you know how you hardly even think about it. Getting to that point takes a little practice.

GRANDMA:

One of her grandchildren decided it would be a neat idea to buy her a glide ride for her seventy-sixth birthday and she is quite excited about it.

Getting into a glider is not like getting into a 747. The edge of the cockpit is high off the ground and although there is a small foot peg for boarding, it does require a degree of manual dexterity. This is no easy task for the elderly or the handicapped.

The whole family is present to witness this flight and with a few of them to help me we get her into the front seat of the glider and belted in securely. The tow plane comes, we are hooked up and off we go for what I hope will be a pleasant experience for her.

She really is getting a kick out of the ride and so am I. She informs me that we just flew over the Smith farm, she knows it's their place because she can see the quince tree in the back yard. This cracks me up. The flight comes to an end too soon; I was really enjoying it.

All her children and grandchildren are there and they surround the ship after we roll to a stop. We get her out of the thing and it is time for the obligatory photo shoot. Of course there has to be one of the passenger and pilot together. Over the years I have wondered in how many family photo albums do I appear, standing next to a passenger in front of a glider with a big grin on my face? I love this kind of demo.

It never ceases to amaze me what some people's concept of a demo flight is. On several occasions I have answered the phone in the office and some young sounding voice tells me they want to give a glider ride as a birthday present to their grandmother. I explain about the cost, how high we will tow them, how long the flight will probably last, how safe it is and stuff like that. I figure I have pretty well covered all the bases when the voice asks a question I never really thought about. "Will someone go up with her or will she go up alone?"

There is a long moment of stunned silence while I try to figure out if they are serious. They are. I carefully explain that she will go up with a licensed highly trained pilot who has over a hundred flights in his logbook. The next question has got to be one of my all time favorites; "Will the glider crash if the wind stops?" I give them an abbreviated course in glider aerodynamics, and after twenty minutes on the phone they are sold.

I don't mind taking the time to sell them; I want everyone to experience the joy of soaring. I really find it hard to believe that someone would actually think we would take this perfectly charming; seventy something lady with slightly blue hair, strap her into the seat of an aircraft and tow her up into the sky, alone. Then after awhile, cut her loose to drift hither and yon and eventually come down somewhere. I wonder if they worry about things like, if it is really windy, will they have to make a long drive to pick grandma up in Cedar Rapids, Iowa.

BORED:

It only happened to me once. The average glider flight with a tow to two thousand feet will last approximately fifteen minutes. If I encounter any lift at all I try to keep them up for thirty minutes.

It was a hot muggy day in August and lift was very scarce and what there was, was very light. I sat there in the back seat sweating and really working hard to give this guy a good ride .He was awfully quiet and I thought perhaps he was becoming ill.

"How do you like this," I asked. "I find this terribly boring" he replied. I couldn't believe my ears. For a moment I contemplated doing some maneuvers that I was sure would empty him like a bucket. I wanted to see if he found that boring but I was afraid that he would mess up my ship. I slammed the spoilers full open, stood the ship up on a wing tip and we were on the ground in less than two minutes. Boring indeed!

DOING TWO THINGS AT THE SAME TIME

She was a little bit on the far side of middle age. A rather large woman wearing sensible shoes, who kept referring to me as "young man." Perhaps "matronly" is the word I am looking for here. Yeah, "matronly," like in a woman's prison.

I have a standard line of patter I use on my demo flights in the hope that the passenger will understand and enjoy the flight as much as possible.

As we passed over the end of the runway I said, "We are climbing out now and at two hundred feet we will be at our safety altitude. If for any reason we should have to abort the take off over that altitude we will just turn back to the field and land." I felt sure she would like to have this information. She said, "I wish you wouldn't talk so much and pay a little more attention to your flying."

All those suppressed memories from long ago of Sister Mary Flagellation came flooding back over me. I swear I heard myself whimper. "My God" I thought, "how lucky for me to be sitting behind her instead of in front."

If I were sitting in front of her, she would surely have noticed that I was chewing gum and made me spit it out. She probably would have smacked me up alongside the head too.

MOTORCYCLE MAMA

If I ever wanted to make a "Hells Angels" type of motion picture he would have been in it. He was in full rig, boots, leather chaps, hat and vest. He had tattoos all over his big hairy arms, chains hanging here and there and metal studs sticking out all over. His hair was long, and his beard was even longer. He must have stood six feet four inches without his boots on. The gal with him would have been in the same movie too.

"Ron" he said, "I want you to meet my woman, Sparkle." "How do you do Miss Sparkle" I said, trying to be as polite as possible. "Ron, I want you to give Sparkle a real nice ride and make sure it is a (long) one too." Most glider flights without the aid of thermal lift will last about 15 minutes and I don't think her boy friend wanted to hear about that. If ever I prayed for a thermal that was the time. I prayed to Saint Jude, patron saint of hopeless cases. We got Sparkle strapped in and we were off. Saint Jude must have heard my prayer because we got off tow at two thousand and hooked into a boomer. Soon we were at four grand and I stopped sweating.

It is company policy to limit demo flights to thirty minutes but I gave Sparkle forty-five. She really seemed to enjoy the flight. We landed and he was there as we rolled to a stop. She was happy, he was happy and I was extremely happy. They thanked me, jumped on their hog and roared out of my life forever.

I still wonder how I would have explained a twelve-minute flight to him.

BIG MAMA

As we rolled to a stop my passenger, a large, middle aged man told me his wife would be going up with me next and here she comes now. I followed his glance and saw what was possibly the biggest woman I had ever seen. She was walking towards the glider accompanied by one of the owners of the operation and a line boy. The owner helped the man out of the ship and then he and the line boy huffed and puffed and pushed and pulled on various body parts and finally succeeded in getting the ample lady into the ship.

Unfortunately they got her in backwards. She was standing in the front seat looking at me. Her husband was enjoying the proceedings immensely. He was laughing and cracking jokes. They told her to turn around and sit down. This was no easy maneuver for her. She was quite jovial about the whole thing and said, " I think I need a bigger airplane." The line boy, silver tongued lad that he was said, "Lady this is the biggest ship we got."

Now her husband really cracked up. I thought he would fall on the ground and start to roll around. "Howard," the lady said," If you ever tell anyone what that kid said, you will get nothing but wieners and beans for a week."

As luck would have it the Cessna 150/150 tow ship pulled up close, took a good look at us, made a 180 turn and stopped. I could see the line boy and the pilot talking and gesturing. Then the tow plane made 90 degree turn and headed across to take another glider waiting to be towed. The line boy came back to us and said, "We are gonna get a tow plane with a bigger engine. Howard forgot all about the wieners and beans and was laughing and slapping his knees.

We finally got airborn and completed the flight. The lady was happy, I was happy, and Howard was still laughing.

I DON'T FEEL SMALL BUT I GUESS I AM

Because I am the smallest and lightest pilot on the field I get all the biggest and heaviest passengers. All the other pilots get the cute young thing in short shorts and halter top but not me, oh no, never.

I was sitting at the picnic table shooting the breeze with the other pilots when this positively huge man came into view and went into the office. All the other guys started to snicker and point their fingers at me. They knew what was going to happen.

The manager poked his head out of the window and said, "Ron, will you come in here please." I got up and went inside, everybody followed. Center of gravity charts for various gliders were consulted, gross weight estimates were made, glider volume was discussed. It was decided that we would put him into the back seat of an SGS 2-33A and I would fly from the front seat. Everybody went outside.

All the seat cushions were removed from the back seat. His left leg was loaded first and then by pushing on his head we got the main part of his body inside. His right leg was still outside and try as may we just could not get it inside.

Someone mentioned that they didn't think the Federal Aviation Administration would like it if we flew around with the door open and the passengers' leg hanging out. I can't recall of ever reading anything that expressly prohibited flying with a portion of the passenger hanging out but I sure didn't think it would look right.

A discussion ensued as to what effect this configuration would have on the flight characteristics of the aircraft. It was thought by some that the disrupted airflow would cause the tail section to buffet. Others felt that the glide ratio would suffer greatly and I wondered if we would have any glide ratio at all.

Finally we had to turn the guy down. He was very disappointed until someone remembered that our competition had a three-place glider and perhaps they could accommodate him. He left with a small glimmer of hope that he might still get a glider ride. I wonder if he ever did?

HOW MUCH WOULD YOU PAY TO GET SICK

It was a really windy day. It was blowing thirty miles per hour but it was right down the runway and the velocity was constant.

We had very little business and I was bored. I wanted to fly. I hate it when I show up to work and sit around all day. The next customer was a demo and he wasn't supposed to show up till three o'clock. At least he had signed up for a mile high ride in a high performance ship.

The passenger showed up on time and as we walked down the line towards the glider he told me now much he had looked forward to this flight. He was very enthusiastic and this made me happy.

We took off and started our long tow to 5280.feet. I kept up a line of patter pointing this out and telling him about that. At first he seemed to be enjoying it but as the tow progressed he became quieter and quieter, too quiet, bad sign.

I finally asked him how he liked the ride? If you have to ask, you really don't want to know. He said he was surprised how bumpy it was and asked why we turned so much? I explained that the bumpiness was caused by the wind creating turbulence and we turned because we had to stay behind the tow plane.

We finally reached our goal of one mile high and I pulled the release knob to separate us from the tow plane. I made a ninety-degree turn to the right to clear the tow. "Please don't do anymore turns," he said. I tried to figure out how we could get back to the field without turning, it was three miles behind us and about a mile to our right. "I don't feel so good, do you have an air sick bag"? I handed him a bag.

Looking out the right side of the canopy, I noticed a road running parallel to the leading edge of the right wing. It wasn't moving backwards or forwards, we were just hanging there in the sky like a big kite. The wind velocity must have been 60 MPH and it was right on our nose. We burned off 3500 feet and never moved an inch.

I made a big gentle turn to get headed back to the field and a few more to line up with the runway. As soon as we landed he jumped out of the ship and was gone. I felt so sorry for him. He had just spent $114.00 and all he got for it was sick.

MY HERO

Maybe I am just too trusting. If someone tells me something I see no reason not to believe it, I take whatever they say to be gospel truth. Boy, have I ever been surprised at times!

As I belted the demo into the front seat I asked him if he was a pilot? "Yes I am" he replied. I asked him what type of aircraft he had flown. "Well, once I flew a Fokker Dr-1." My mouth dropped open. "Wow, you mean the German tri-plane, the world war one fighter plane, one like the Red Baron flew"? "Yep," he said.

Isn't it amazing, I thought, the people you get as demos out here. Who would have ever expected this, average looking fellow too, I thought. Come to think of it now, most of the pilots I ever met were rather average looking.

"God, I envy you," I said. "I would give anything to have done that." He smiled a little smile that said, "Yeah kid, I know you would." I felt very fortunate to have this man as a passenger. I couldn't wait to tell the other guys about this. They would never believe me. I asked him how he prepared himself to fly such a tricky aircraft? One doesn't take dual instruction in a Dr-1. I wondered what other aircraft he had flown to prepare himself for the first flight and so I asked him.

"Oh, it wasn't that complicated," he said, "I just belted in, fired up and took off. I had a radio with me and the regular pilot told me what pedal to push and stuff like that."

I felt like jerking the guy out of there and telling him to go into the bathroom, put a bar of soap in your mouth for lying and don't come out till I tell you. Sister Benidicta used to do that to kids in her class who lied, but she made them stand in the coat room where she could keep an eye on them and make sure they didn't take the soap out of their mouth.

WOMEN SAY THE DARNDEST THINGS

Art Linkletter said, "Kids say the darndest things." Well they aren't the only ones. I have already said that I sometimes think that women are the more adventuresome of the two sexes. I also think they are often more frank and forward in their talk. I have had women passengers say things to me in the cockpit that really surprised me.

I always try to give a good demo flight. If there is any lift at all I will work it and stay up for a half-hour. If we get up high I will ask them if they would enjoy some aerobatics.

As soon as we got off tow at two thousand feet we hit a real boomer and in no time at all we were going through 4000. I thought this would be a good time to do some wing overs, some stalls and maybe if that went well we could do some push overs. I said, "Well, here we are with plenty of altitude and we still have lots of time, would you like to fool around a little?" She replied, " "Its fine with me but we mustn't let my husband know." At first I was a little surprised and then I began to laugh. I assumed she was joking. Still I wonder, if I hadn't been firmly strapped down in the seat behind her and busy flying the glider, would she still have said that to me? I'll never know.

WAS IT GOOD FOR YOU?

By the time we got to the up wind end of the runway I knew she was really going to enjoy this flight. She was laughing and giggling and saying how great it was.

On the tow to two thousand feet she said she wanted an exciting flight. "I want it all, do everything," she said. Well on tow there isn't a whole heck of a lot I could do. After all we were hooked to the tow plane. I did do a box tow, which means describing a box around the tow planes wake, and was rewarded with more giggles and laughter.

Off tow we hooked into a real good thermal and I climbed to slightly over forty five hundred in a short time. I didn't ask her if she wanted to do some aerobatics, I knew. Some real tight wingovers produced laughter. Some deep stalls produced screams of delight. By the time we got to push overs she had her knees drawn up to her chest, her head flung back over the seat back, arms flailing around in the canopy, and she was shrieking, "Yes, Oh God, Yes"!

This type of behavior did nothing for me except spur me on to even greater aerobatic endeavors. For the first time in my life I actually contemplated flying the ship inverted, just to see what effect this would have on her. A quick glance at the altimeter told me I didn't have enough altitude for that. We were burning it up like crazy. If I had another thousand feet I swear to God I would have tried.
We landed, rolled to a stop and I helped the gal out of the ship.

"You know" she said, "this is a whole lot better than sex." Somehow I believe she really meant that.

DRUNKS

It was overcast and a light drizzle was falling. The blowing wind made it feel colder than it was. All our students and demos had called to cancel.

We had the furnace going in the trailer and were sitting around talking, doing some hanger flying, then the phone rang and because I was closest to it I picked it up. A slurred voice on the other end said, "Shay, I wanna go for a glider ride. I was sposed go for a parachute jump but can't, so now I wanna go for a ride."

I explained that this wasn't a good day for a ride. I told him it would probably be a very short ride and surely he would enjoy it more on a nicer day. "Don't care, wanna go now." I asked where he was calling from? He told me he was calling from "J Js." Where else I thought. "J Js" is one of the two bars in the town of Hinckley, Illinois.

I really didn't want to go out into the cold and damp, untie a glider, pre flight it and then take someone in his condition up for one demo. Then I would have to tie the ship down again. It just wasn't worth it. No matter how hard I tried to talk him out of it he just wouldn't listen. I finally said "O.K., come on out."

I left the warm trailer grumbling to myself. The tow pilot was none too happy about it either and expressed his displeasure as he followed me out the door. I could hear his bitching and moaning half the way to the hanger to get the tow ship ready.

The pre-flight was just completed when the customer showed up. He came around the corner of the trailer. He had a cigarette in one hand and a can of beer in the other. The course he was steering was none too steady. After I introduced myself I told him to lose the butt and the beer. The can described a perfect arch in the air, spewing beer the whole way and landed ten rows back in the cornfield. So much for ecology. The butt fell to the ground and I stamped that out.

Drunk as he was he managed to get aboard without too much hassle. I got him buckled in and we took off. The flight was a short one. I sure as hell didn't do any thing to make it any longer than it had to be.

It was a real job getting him out of the ship. I inhaled so much booze breath I was beginning to get tipsy. Then he informed me he would go back to the car and try and talk his girl friend into taking a ride.

My spirits brightened somewhat, at least I would get two flights for my efforts and surely she couldn't be as bad as he was. Wrong. She was perhaps a little drunker than he was.

I don't think I have ever seen a drunken woman before. My life certainly wasn't what you would call sheltered. I spent four years in the Navy and had visited some pretty rough ports but I don't recall having ever had this experience before. Someone once told me that there is nothing worse than a drunken woman. Drunken men are no prize that's for sure but this gal was making a believer out of me. Not only was she severely inebriated, she had a bad case of "Potty Mouth."

I more or less poured her into the front seat and got her belted in. This procedure elicited all sorts of lewd remarks about belts, bondage and she hoped I would be gentle with her and on and on.

The flight was even shorter than that of her friend. When we landed she told him all the things we did in the air, none of which had anything to do with flying. I told him to get her out of the glider. I didn't want anymore to do with her.
They staggered off the field to the parking lot and drove off. I wonder if they made to wherever they were going? I didn't care what they did to themselves but sure hoped they didn't kill some innocent people.

Until that time I had never taken a drunken person up for a flight and I certainly never will again. If they can't walk straight, they can't fly.

SWEET SIXTEEN WITH A BROKEN HEART

Her parents brought her out to the airport and told me the story. She had just got back from a Civil Air Patrol Encampment where she had elected to learn to fly a glider. It seems all her classmates soloed except her. They wanted to know if I could work with her and get her soloed?

It must be tough being that young and having all that peer pressure to bear. It sort of put me in a spot though. I really wanted to help this kid but what if she just didn't have it? What if she was that one in a hundred that would never learn to fly no matter how hard we tried?

We went up for a series of three flights and I felt sure I could do it. So we worked together. I don't really remember now how many flights it took but it wasn't all that many before I climbed out of the back seat, signed her license and logbook off for solo. I sent her off on the flight that no student will ever forget.

She flew the thing without a hitch; even the landing was perfect. Her parents were there and congratulations were passed around. Everyone was all smiles but her's seemed to be bigger than our's. She went away and I never saw her again. I guess it was just one of those things she had to do before getting on with the rest of her life.

The day I sign a person off for solo is the time I realize how much responsibility this job really has. Kids come out to the field with their parents because the state says they aren't old enough to drive. Then one day I must decide if they can fly. It is my name in their logbook. I am responsible, me and only me. I put my name on the dotted line, they solo, then they jump in the car again with mom and she drives them home.

THE NATURAL

He was young, maybe 16 or 17. He was possibly the best student I have ever had. Once or twice a week he would come out to the field and we would go up for the standard three flights. His progress was amazing and I felt he was a natural.

As the time grew near for him to solo I kept telling him that he had to pass the pre solo written test before I would turn him lose. I would ask him if he had studied his books and he assured me he had. I felt sure he could do it, no problem. He kept showing up for more lessons. I didn't know what to do with him anymore. On one flight I told the tow pilot to take us up to 2000 feet over the next town about three and a half miles to the west of the field.

At 2000 I pulled the release knob and told him to find an airport and land, but don't land at the home field. He calmly made a few circles and then spotted the field I knew was there. He set up the pattern perfectly and made a good landing. The tow plane came back for us shortly and towed us out of there.

I never asked a pre-solo student to do what I had just asked him to do. When we got back to the field I told him he was just wasting his money and my time and that I would solo him as soon as he took the written test. Once again he assured me he would take the test soon. Then he stopped coming out to the field.

His mother was also a student of mine and after awhile when it became apparent that there was a problem, I asked her why her son wasn't showing up anymore? She told me," He never ever wants you to get out of the back seat." I couldn't believe what she just told me. Most young students can't wait for old blabbermouth to get out of the glider so they can finally fly with some peace and quiet. Not this one!

It was then for the first time that I realized just how much faith and trust people put in the instructor in the back seat.

Once while waiting for a tow, the lady in the front seat said," You know, I have known my family doctor all my life but if I had to have a serious operation I don't think I would trust him to do it. Now here I am with you, a total stranger, and I am trusting you to fly me around in an airplane without a motor."

AIRLINE PILOTS

Over the years I have had a number of airline pilots as students. It always amazed me that here is this fifty-year-old man who flies this humungous, extremely complex 747 between Chicago and Honolulu and he wants me to teach him to fly a glider. This seems to me to be analogous to the captain of the Queen Elizabeth II asking me to teach him how to row a boat.

Every aircraft is different, each has its own idiosyncrasies. They all have one thing in common however; no matter how large or small, no matter how complex or simple, they are all capable of hitting the ground with enough force to kill you. The only difference is the big ones make big holes and the little ones make little holes.

The first thing I learned was that not all airline pilots are created equal. Some of these guys are real propellerheads. They love anything aeronautical and some of them fly for the airlines because it is a job, just like being a dentist or a lawyer. I never had the latter type as a student because he wouldn't be interested in taking glider lessons anyhow, but I have met them. Even though they may all be airline pilots they do have different skill levels just like you and me or anybody else.

I once had two young airline pilots as students at the same time. They were buddies and would always show up at the field together. Both of these guys were good but I always felt that one was slightly better than the other. As I got to know them better I thought I discovered the reason why. The one I felt was a little better was a true propellerhead. He told me he had at one time or other owned an AT-6, a Bucker Jungmann and several other really neat airplanes. The other flew for the airlines period.

When I am assigned an airline pilot as a student, the captain and I stroll down the line to an old 2-33A trainer and pop the canopy open.

"Wow! He says, there isn't much to one of these things is there?" I tell him he is right and I point out to him that one of the things missing is a throttle. He gets my point.

He is used to being surrounded by hundreds of dials, knobs, switches and levers and now he is faced with an instrument panel with just a few. In a training glider there is an altimeter, airspeed indicator, compass, variometer and last but not least a yaw string.

The yaw string is the simplest and possibly the most necessary instrument of all. It consists of a four inch piece of yarn taped to the centerline of the canopy or tied to a vertical mast on the nose of the glider. To fly the glider properly, the yaw string must be centered at all tines no matter what maneuver you are performing with the exception of slips. It is the one instrument most students have trouble with.

I have never seen a glider without a yaw string. It doesn't matter if the glider is a lowly basic trainer or a $65,000.00 latest and greatest competition ship. They all have them.

On a few occasions I have taken off and then discovered the yaw string was missing or fouled and I feel naked with out the darned thing. I can fly without it of course but it doesn't take me long to get a piece of yarn and a piece of tape and stick it back on.

So the captain and I take off and the lessons begin. So far I have never met an airline pilot who didn't really enjoy soaring. It is back to basics for them, real stick and rudder flying. A far cry from what they are used to and they really love it.

THE DAY WE CLOSED RTE 30

It was about 3:30 P.M. on one of those typical hot, humid, Midwest July days. The temperature was in the high 90's and the humidity wasn't far behind. It was the year of one of the worst droughts the Midwest had ever seen. The creeks were just about dry and the land was parched. Dust devils marched across the brown landscape. We set a record for the number of days over 100 degrees.

It was a really busy day and I was getting pretty frazzled. The back seat of a training glider was not a pleasant place to be on a day like this and I couldn't wait for the day to end.

My student was a Chinese fellow whom I had flown with before. He was a pretty good student but I couldn't get him to call out two hundred feet as we went through that altitude on the initial tow. This is the altitude you must attain before you can release from the tow plane and make a 180-degree turn back to the field for any reason. Anything less than 200 feet and you landed straight ahead with minor turns to miss the cows and tractors.

On the first two flights he forgot to call out two hundred feet. We were just about to take our third tow when I remembered something. Earlier that week I had two glider pilots from New Zealand who did something I had never seen before. They would keep their left hand on the tow release knob until we reached 200 and then yell out "Two hundred feet" and take their hand off the knob.

Great! I thought, perhaps this will help. The only trouble was that something distracted me before we started the tow and I forgot to tell the student. We had just become airborn when I remembered and said," put your hand on the release knob and-----"-BANG-he pulled it! I couldn't believe it! We were less than one hundred feet in the air. I took the controls and set it down in a bean field.

I bolted out of the cockpit, threw my hat on the ground, stomped around in the beans and said some very uninstructor like things. I could just envision all the huffing and puffing, sweating and straining, busted and bleeding knuckles that were about to come. We would have to disassemble the glider, hand carry all the heavy parts to the nearest road, load it onto a trailer, haul it back to the field, unload it, assemble it and tie it down before it was dark. The mosquitoes would eat us alive. I was not a happy camper.

I finally calmed down enough and looked at the student. He was still sitting in the cockpit under the bubble canopy in the blazing sun, sweat streaming out of every pore. I told him to get out and get under the wing in the shade while I went for help.

Then another pilot who had witnessed the whole ugly affair showed up and I sent him to muster all the help he could find. Soon we had a goodly sized crew and it was decided that maybe we could get the glider through between the nearby farmers barn and other out buildings, down his drive way, across his front yard and out onto state route 30. That way maybe we wouldn't have to go through the hassle of disassembling the damn thing.

We planed to push it down route 30 to a dirt road at the end of the runway, then down the road, lift it over a barbed wire fence and there we would be, back on the field again. It sounded like a winner to me. Anything, as long as we didn't have to take that pig apart.

Someone was going to have to tell the farmer our plan and get his permission to carry it out. Guess who? So with hat in hand I timidly tapped on the back door. When I explained the situation he was almost as unhappy as I was. What with the drought he wasn't going to have much of a crop anyhow and now we were about to destroy some of that. I told him we had insurance and that calmed him down somewhat. He gave us permission.

It was a tight squeeze but by turning the glider this way and that, tipping the wing down and the tail up, we finally ended up with the ship in the farmers' back yard. We pushed it down the drive and ended up with the thing in his front yard. We were all covered with sweat and dust.

There was no way I was going to try pushing the glider down route 30 without somehow getting traffic stopped first. I could just see an eighteen wheeler, going through a glider wing at sixty-five miles per hour. The farmer let me use his phone so I called the Hinckley police department. They said it was out of their jurisdiction and that I should call the County Sheriff. They did however send a squad car out to join in the festivities.

I called the County Sheriff and he told me it was out of his jurisdiction and that I should call the State Highway Patrol. They also sent a squad car out. I called the State Highway Patrol, "BINGO"; they sent two patrol cars out.

We had four squad cars sitting on the shoulder of the road, all of them with their lights flashing. There were about a dozen more cars parked there, some of them belonging to helpers and some to the curious. Traffic was beginning to pile up. I could see the drivers and passengers pointing and talking. I could just imagine what was being said: "My God Martha! How did that big airplane ever land in that small yard?"

I explained what we wanted to do to the senior state trooper. He listened to me intently and them said, "Say, can't you take that thing apart, put it on a trailer and haul it back to the field?" I felt lightheaded, my vision blurred, my knees began to buckle, my mind raced. Then I said," No sir, that would void the warranty."

The officer looked me straight in the eyes for what must have been a full four seconds and seemed like four hours. I felt faint again.

"OK," he said, "We will close the highway down, but I will have to radio in for permission." To this day I don't know if he really believed me or did he just think it was one of the most unique lies he had ever heard. Perhaps he thought anyone who could come up with an excuse like that deserves to be cut a little slack.

Now all the officers got in their respective police cars and got on their radios and talked and talked. I was beginning to think I might loose the game yet. I don't know how far up the chain of command this thing went. George Bush was Vice President then and it may have gotten to him. If I ever meet George I will ask him.

Finally one patrol car was dispatched one mile east and one went one mile west. The traffic came to a halt. The glider was pushed out onto the highway. What a beautiful sight it was, rolling down the centerline, six hearty lads pushing and pulling. God! I wished I had a camera.

By six that evening she was tied in her spot on the field. Not a scratch on her. I went home, took a nice long shower and had a few beers.

I AM A NICE GUY

I don't know where we got that stuff, that spool of towline. I strongly suspect it was purchased at K-MART on a "blue light special. The line seemed to be composed of reconstituted spider web. It had no strength at all.

As far as instructors go I will probably let a student go a lot farther than most. I have heard some students say of other instructors, " I don't know if I am flying the glider or he is?" Believe me, with me they knew.

For some reason that day every student I got was at the point in their lessons where they had to be taught "slack line recovery." Also for some reason that day I kept getting the same Polish tow pilot. Most glider pilots really liked the guy. If he encountered lift he would do his best to keep you in it.

He would practically stand the tow ship up on its wing tip and go zipping around in some really tight circles. Pilots loved him, students were terrified.

I told him again before we towed that we would be doing slack line. He didn't look all that enthused at the prospect. Maybe it was because I had already broken two towlines with him that day. Practicing slack line really gives the tow pilot a workout. His tail is constantly being pulled this way and that and he has to fight to maintain control of the ship.

To do slack line recovery, the instructor gets high on tow off to one side and dives the ship to make the line go slack then he demonstrates how to remove it. The slack forms a bow in the line off to one side and I always tell the student to turn away from the bow and to release if the bow should ever look like it was going to touch the glider.

After demonstrating the technique twice to the student, I told him I would get some slack and this time he could take it out. After getting a good bow I told the student to "take it." The student immediately turned into the bow. I grabbed the controls but it was too late. The line arched towards us and draped itself over the wings leading edge.

I pulled the release knob and saw the line do something I had never seen it do before. It skittered out along the length of the wing and made several wraps around the outrigger tip wheel. For a second I thought, "this glider is not going to fly very good going sideways. If the tow plane doesn't release we are both going to be in trouble big time."

There was a sickening lurch and the ship yawed to the right. I saw the tow plane buck. With a loud bang the 7/16 inch spring steel outrigger wheel on the wings tip snapped off clean. I guess that towline wasn't some of the "blue light special."

Later that evening I walked into the office and there was my Polish tow pilot friend. In a heavy Polish accent he said. "Ron, you are a nice guy but I am not going to tow for you anymore." Of course he did tow for me many times after that and we remained friends but at the time I think he was dead serious. I thought it was hilarious.

TEST PILOT

It was a slick looking ship, two place, all fiberglass, plush interior, I really hated it. I called it the "Plastic Cow." Maybe it was just me. Maybe I wasn't big enough or strong enough to fly it properly. I was forever on the rudder pedals. I felt like I was pedaling it across the sky.

So they told me to take this fellow up for a field check ride. A field check can be a simple thing. All you have to do is determine if the testee can fly the glider safely. It usually takes one flight but if the testee does something to arouse suspicion, it can take all afternoon and then he or she might not get signed off.

This guy was real good. After awhile he asked me how I liked the ship and I told him I really didn't like it at all. I mentioned that I had to continually use the rudder pedals to keep the yaw string straight. He mentioned that the newer models had a slightly larger rudder. That made me feel good, but I wondered how he had acquired that information?

Later I found out that he was a test pilot for the company that built the glider. That made me feel even better.

UNDUE CONCERN

It was a sunny Sunday afternoon and I had scheduled the single place Schweizer 1-26 to build some time towards my private pilot glider license. It was extremely busy that day and I was anxious to fly, as all students are. Sitting in the ship sweating, and all ready to go, I watched glider after glider being towed off. Finally it was my turn.

Schweizer I-26E

The right wing was down and as the line boy hooked up the towrope, he asked me if I wanted him to run my wing? I declined his offer, as I wanted to get some practice taking off without a wing runner to keep the wings level.

The tow plane pulled the line taunt and after going through the check-list one more time, I closed and locked the canopy and gave the thumbs up signal to the line boy to start the tow. The line boy in turn signaled the tow plane to go.

Just as the ship began to move I caught some movement out of the corner of my right eye. Someone was running towards the glider along my right wings leading edge. This nut jumped over the towrope and almost cleared the now rapidly advancing left wing, almost!

I couldn't believe what was happening and at that stage of training I did not respond quick enough to pull the tow release. I like to think that now I would have, although I don't think it would have done much good. The left wing caught him knee high. He executed a beautiful cartwheel over the top of the wing.

I should have aborted the tow right there. Again it is something I like to think I would have done now. "Stupid shit," I thought. The controls felt all right so I proceeded with the flight.

After getting off tow and flying around awhile I became more and more concerned about the accident. "Gee!" I thought, "I wonder if that guy is all right, did he break his neck, will he sue, maybe he is dead?" The longer I flew the more badly I felt.

The flight didn't last all that long. When I landed I hurriedly pushed the ship off the runway, secured it and ran into the office. Sure enough he was in there having a serious discussion with the manager of the field, who also happened to be this fellow's instructor. There were a lot of people milling about in there and it was too noisy to get the drift of their conversation. I sat down in the corner and waited.

He finally did leave and I went up to the counter to speak to the manager. I looked around cautiously and in a very low and confidential voice I asked, "How is that guy doing?" The manager looked around cautiously and in a very low and confidential voice said, "Doesn't use enough rudder in the turns."

NEVER TRUST A TOW PILOT WEARING A CRASH HELMET

It was the fall season and most of our regular tow pilots who all want to be airline pilots had gone back to college. Some other pilots were hired to replace them.

I was a fresh new private pilot with very little time in my logbook. Sitting in the almost new SGS 1-26 I saw the new tow pilot come out of the office and climb into the tow plane. He was wearing a crash helmet, commonly referred to as a "Brain Bucket." "Odd." I thought.

The line boy who hooked me up told me to, " watch out for that guy, he is wild." Apparently the day before he had started to tow a glider before the proper signal was given. Several people who were standing in front of the ship taking pictures had to dive for cover. I decided to pay lots of attention to the tow.

As it turned out the tow was quite normal and I encountered lift at 2000 feet and released. It was a nice flight and as I entered the landing pattern I checked for traffic, nothing on downwind, nothing on base, nothing on final. Great! I thought, I am number one in the pattern. On base leg my attention was directed to the runway. There was lots of action down there, lots of people getting ready to commit aviation but the runway was clear. Just as I turned final a dark shadow was cast over my canopy. Not far above me and somewhat off to my right, the tow plane went sailing by. Where did he come from I thought?

The wind was blowing from the right and it drifted the towline over my glider. There was a terrible clankity, clank, clank, noise and my ship was jerked about violently. It was all over in a second. The glider was still flyable but the left side of the canopy had turned a milky white.

After landing the thing, I got out and inspected the damage. There were quite a few dents in the aluminum skin. Running my hand over the canopy it came away with what looked like the stuff we used to put on the Christmas tree when I was a kid, we called it "Angel Hair." The canopy was still clear underneath. I guess the stuff came from the towline.

I went to the office and told the manager what had happened. We went out and gave the glider a thorough inspection. After looking at the dents, it was determined that the towline had apparently wrapped completely around the fuselage. We wiped the Angel Hair off the canopy and checked the ship for structural damage; it was declared airworthy.

When I think of all the places where that tow line could have jammed and what would have happened if it did, I counted my lucky stars. At the altitude the incident took place we would have both ended up going in. It was just dumb luck, nothing more.

The whole affair taught me a valuable lesson, don't expect everyone to fly the pattern even though they are supposed to. Look where you least expect to see someone. Most of all, don't trust tow pilots wearing crash helmets.

EVERYBODY WANTS TO GO TO HEAVEN BUT NOBODY WANTS TO DIE

At first I thought I would call this section DEATH but I figured that would be too morbid. It is about death however.

We were sitting around shooting the breeze one day when I came out with the old saying; "If God had meant man to fly, He would have given him wings." Somebody replied, "No Ron, if God had meant man to fly, He would have given him more money." Everyone laughed. Then one of the pilots said something I will never forget. He said, "If God told me that if I didn't stop flying I would die in an airplane, I wouldn't stop flying." Pretty strong words, I thought. Still, as horrible as those last few moments must be, it must be better than some other ways of dying I have seen.

I have a brass plaque on which are engraved the words, "There are old pilots and bold pilots but there are no old bold pilots." I wonder if I shouldn't have some plaques made up that say, "If you are an old pilot, you are a lucky pilot." I really wonder if there are any pilots around with a couple of thousand hours in their logbooks who wouldn't have to truthfully say that they have been damn lucky a time or two? I know I would have to admit it and I know a few others that would too.

On a warm sunny Sunday morning I sat at the picnic table on the field and laughed and joked with a young pilot who was the manager of the field that year, his name was Kevin. I really liked the kid. He was in his early twenties and full of aviation hopes and dreams. A couple of days later he was just a memory. His student was a friend of mine also. I lost two friends on the same day in the same airplane. It doesn't seem possible they are gone.

The only reason I went out to the field that day was to clean some spark plugs with the spark plug cleaning machine they have.

Citabria Township

When I arrived something seemed strange. The door to the office was open and the radio was on but no one was there. There wasn't a car in the parking lot. I started to walk towards the hanger when I saw the cute little gal from Denmark; she was one of the pilots for the jump school, coming my way. I said "Hi" and asked her how she was doing. She said she wasn't doing very well and then she told me one of the tow planes crashed. I asked her who was flying and she said she didn't know. I asked her where it had crashed and she told me and said they wouldn't let anyone near there. I had to find out.

I took route 30 west to a gravel road where there were a lot of emergency vehicles, parked the car and started to walk down the road. About half way back a young lady in some kind of uniform said, "I'm sorry sir but you can't go beyond this point." I don't remember what I said as I brushed on by. I didn't want to go to the crash sight, I knew what I would find there and I didn't want to see that. I just had to find someone who could tell me who was in the plane. As I got closer I saw the owner of the jump school and he told me the "Citabria" tow-plane went in on a training flight. He said he didn't know who the student was but the instructor was Kevin. I couldn't believe it. Back at the field I found out the student was a friend of mine named "Allen." That made me even sadder than I was before.

When I got back to the field, Tim who was a tow pilot and a very close friend of Kevin and his family, was there. One look at him and I knew how he was taking it. He told me he had called Kevin's mom and told her that Kevin was involved in an accident. I guess he just couldn't bring himself to tell her that he was dead. She was on the way to the field at that time. I didn't want to be around when she got there but every time I started to leave someone would detain me with some question or something.

Then she was there. Tim must have seen her approach from the trailer because he met her first. She said something about, "How bad is he?" Tim didn't say anything, he didn't have to. I saw her knees start to go and she made a strange sound. I guess only a mother who just finds out that her young son is dead could make that sound. They took her into the trailer. The padre was there.

A couple of days later I walked back that well trod path of broken corn. It ended at a hole in the ground. I don't know why I did it; I don't know what I expected to find. There was an odd smell in the air and the flies were thick. In the bottom of the hole was a fresh cut rose.

The Federal Aviation Administration attributes an awful lot of accidents to pilot error. It sometimes seems to me that the first error a pilot makes is untying the damn airplane. If he would just leave the thing anchored to the ground nothing would happen, maybe.

You don't have to fly in an airplane to get killed. My nieces' son, I guess that would make him my grand nephew, was killed in an automobile. He was driving down a country road and a tree fell on his car and killed him.

One Sunday after mass was over and my wife and I had just left the church a strange thing happened. A news vendor would station himself outside the church every Sunday morning and I walked over to buy a paper. Just then I heard a sound like a string of firecrackers going off. I turned to see a very large tree fall on an automobile.

The people in the front seat had eyes as big as silver dollars. Lucky for them they were in the front seat because the back seat was smashed flat. The fire department was called and they had to use the "Jaws of Life" to extract them from what remained of their car.

The tree, which must have been 50 feet high, was in full leaf and a beautiful specimen. I thought it surely would be around a long time after I was gone. That tree was completely hollow inside, it was rotten in the center but looked perfect on the outside.

I wonder if anyone keeps statistics on how many people per year, in the United States of America, are killed by trees? I wonder how it would compare to aviation fatalities?

When taken in the broader context, flying is probably quite safe. When the customer on the phone asks if it is safe to go up in an airplane without an engine, I tell them the most dangerous part of taking a ride out here is the drive out to the field. I have heard it said that one in every ten cars coming at you on the other side of the road is being driven by someone who has had too much to drink. That is pretty scary stuff.

I guess I am a fatalist. I believe that when your time is up it's up. It doesn't matter what you might be doing at that time.

FEAR

The "CATERPILLAR CLUB" is a very exclusive club. It cost five dollars for a lifetime membership and with that you get a neat little pin to wear on your lapel and a certificate suitable for framing. It isn't the cost that makes this club exclusive; it is the initiation, it's a bitch.

During WWII the "Security Parachute Co." awarded a pin to any pilot who saved his life with a parachute. The pin was in the shape of a caterpillar because parachutes were made of silk and caterpillars made silk. For many years after the war they continued to award that pin.

I don't believe anyone can actually predict how he or she will behave in a fearful situation. Until it happens, you just don't know. I always thought that if something really bad happens to me in an aircraft, I will do three things in rapid succession, scream, mess my pants and pass out.

Then one day something really bad happened to me in an aircraft and I didn't behave at all like I thought I would. I can't say I was really disappointed. It wasn't like, "Ho hum, another day at the office"; it was just that I was very busy. I had lots of things to do and a very short time to do them in and it all had to be done right the first time. The landscape was getting larger by the second. A little while later I was standing in a bean field with a used parachute balled up in my arms. I don't believe I had any fear while all this was happening. I do know I had trouble sleeping for awhile after that. It took a lot of booze to get sleepy.

There are certain scenes that are forever etched in my memory and I can see them as though it was yesterday. Things went into slow motion with an almost dreamlike quality. As I drifted to earth under my parachute canopy, the remains of the ship went by to my left. One wing, the entire tail section and the canopy were missing. The ship was doing a slow roll and every time it turned so I could see into the empty cockpit I saw the seat belts waving at me. They seemed to be beckoning to me. It was as though they were saying, "Come back, come back, you have cheated us."

I began to hear a voice saying, "Ron, Ron, are you all right?" It kept repeating it over and over again. I looked all around and couldn't see anyone. I became exasperated and yelled, "Yes, yes, I'm O K." I just wanted to be left alone. Later I found out it was a friend of mine circling over my chute in another glider with the canopy open yelling at me.

Shortly after the incident I went to see the movie, "The Right Stuff." In the opening scene a cocky young Air Force officer drills it in the X-1. The scene of those unwinding dials and the spinning earth were too much for me. I had to put my head between my knees and clamp a hand over my mouth to keep from screaming. That really surprised me. I didn't think that would happen.

I don't think it has changed my life much. I don't think I am a better person for it. I still go to church as much as I did before it happened. I haven't dedicated my life to saving the silk worm.

There are a few things I do differently these days. When I get into a new and different aircraft I pay a whole lot of attention as to how I will get the hell out if I have to leave in a hurry. I have become very found of my parachute and I always wear it when I fly solo, no matter what aircraft I am flying, even the good old SGS 2-33A.

God forbid that something really bad should happen to me in an aircraft again, if it does I am sure I will do three things in rapid succession, scream, mess my pants and pass out.

THREE STAGES

It seems to me that there are three stages to becoming a pilot. This is my own opinion and not necessarily that of the FAA, or even other instructors for that matter.

At first the student is very concerned with control movements. I will explain what we are about to do to execute a maneuver. Then I will execute the maneuver while they follow through on the controls. I may do this a couple of times. Each time after the maneuver I will explain what we have done with the controls and what visual clues to look for. Then I will ask the student to do the maneuver. Inevitably the student will ask, "Well, how much do I move the controls? Like I am going to tell the student to move the stick 2 and 7/8 inches to the left and push the left rudder pedal 3 inches forward. I tell them to forget about what distance to move the controls and to think of it more in the terms of pressure and to apply whatever pressure is necessary to obtain the desired results.

In the second stage they are no longer concerned with control movement or pressures. They are now concerned with outside references in relation to the aircraft. How much the wings are banked and how much the nose is pitched up or down in relation to the horizon. They are continually looking outside to see if the wings are level. That is good at this stage.

In the third and final stage the student has more or less forgotten about wings and nose position. Now they are more concerned with the relationship of their own body to outside references. They now fly to position themselves in space. The wings and nose of the ship have become merely extensions of themselves.

Although they probably won't reach the third and final stage while they are still students, when they do they will be pilots.

STICK TIME

Flying is sometimes referred to as stick time. There is nothing like stick time. The more stick time you get the better pilot you will be. I don't think it really matters much what you get stick time in as long as you get plenty of it. I know a jet fighter is different than an ultralight but flying is flying.

No matter what you fly if you don't do it right you can find yourself in a whole lot of trouble.

One place where stick time is really apparent to an observer is at a radio control flying field. The spectator will soon note that all the novice flyers will be constantly orienting their bodies to the direction of flight of their models. On landing the novice RC pilots will more or less turn their back to the approaching model and then look over their shoulder to guide the plane in.

The expert flyers will stand at the edge of the field and barely move their body no matter what position the model is in. It can be going away, coming towards them, right side up or inverted. They can perform the entire aerobatic routine and barely move. They may have their bodies on the ground but mentally they are in the plane. Stick time.

When I first got my private ticket there were some years when I would get less than ten hours a season, (April to December). An awful lot of time was spent flying with a bad case of "Cotton Mouth." I was running scared.

As my skills improved I learned to catch a thermal and ride it, I got more and more time and things improved. Then I got my commercial license and became a "Demo" pilot and things really got better. I was no longer paying to fly but was getting paid to do it, Granted the pay wasn't all that great but I was really building stick time and acquiring skill. After I got my instructors rating it was not uncommon to log over 100 hours a year in gliders alone. When you consider that most instructional flights last 15 to 20 minutes that is a lot of takeoffs and landings. There are many reasons for a pilot not to get a lot of stick time. Flying is certainly not the least expensive of hobbies. Family responsibilities sometime keep a pilot away from the controls for long periods of time. The weather can be bad for weeks on end. An uncooperative spouse is bad news big time.

I always admire the guy who comes out to the field and is smart enough to take some dual instruction after a long lay off. It is cheap insurance. It may cost him a few dollars but in the long run it is well worth it.

Stick time is very important and although flying is like riding a bicycle, you never forget how to ride one, and you sure can get rusty after awhile.

"HI SAILOR, WANT TO GO FOR A RIDE?"

During the Korean War I spent four years in the Navy. Three of those years I was aboard a submarine operating out of Pearl Harbor in Hawaii.

One of my shipmates was taking flying lessons in an old "Interstate Cadet" based at Honolulu International Airport. He would ask some of us on the sub if we would want to go for a ride in an airplane and of course we all wanted to go. A bunch of us would jump into an old jalopy someone owned and drive him out to the airport. He said he couldn't take us up there because he was only a student pilot and it was against the rules for a student to haul passengers. He was also afraid his instructor would catch him doing it. No problem!

Interstate Cadet

He would jump into the plane and take off and we would jump back into the car and drive to an old abandoned emergency landing field called "Kapapa Field" about ten miles away. At least it was ten miles for him but a good bit farther for us through the mountains. He would be there waiting for us when we arrived.

The ride was something else. It was the same for each one of us. Everyone got treated the same. We drew lots to see who would be lucky and go first. Our friend, the student pilot, would climb the old Interstate to 3500 feet, put the ship into a spin and then pull out low enough to scare the hell out of the natives picking pineapples in the fields below. We thought it was great! Most of us went up for a second ride. The second ride was just like the first one except I think we pulled out a little lower the second time.

I can still hear the sound that old spar made when we pulled out. At the time I didn't know it was the spar making all that noise. I asked my friend about the strange sound and he said, "Aw, I don't know, it does it every time." I'll bet it did!

There was a time in my life that I would jump into an airplane with anyone who would offer me a ride. Funny how things change. If someone offers me a ride now I want to see his or her logbook. I pay a lot of attention to how they fly for the first fifteen minutes or so.

Sometimes I wonder how most young men live long enough to become old men?

BUYING A SHARE

Even though I became a glider pilot before I got my power ticket I did start out in power planes. It happened this way.

When my shipmate, the student pilot who gave us the rides, got his discharge I bought his share in the Interstate Cadet. Ah, the good old days. Of course at the time I didn't know they were the good old days.

Instruction cost $3.50 an hour and that included the plane and fuel. After you soloed all you paid for was fuel and the monthly hanger rent and any other expenses which were split among the seven club members. Except for another shipmate who was also a member I never saw anyone else fly the plane. Still every month the expenses were split seven ways. I wasn't complaining.

My first instructor was a tall lanky fellow about fifty years old. He seemed to be all elbows and knees sitting there behind me in the back seat. He communicated with me through a device called a "Gossport" as I recall. This thing consisted of a pair of earphones, which I wore. These were connected by rubber tubing to a speaking funnel, into which he screamed. He did a lot of that.

I'll never forget my first flight. For some unknown reason I felt that I was a natural born pilot and that this would become apparent to him in very short order. One or two flights, maybe three and I figured he would let me solo. Oh yeah!

We climbed out to about three thousand feet and leveled off. He explained the controls to me and then he pointed out a mountain peak on the far horizon and told me to fly straight and level for it. For the next ten minutes I did what I thought was a superb job of this. About this time I felt a blast of cold air hit me from behind and I looked back. He had the door open, his head hanging out, and he was barfing. He then informed me through the Gossports that in seventeen years of instructing, I was the only student that ever made him sick. That took a little starch out of my sails. To this day I don't really believe he was sick and I think he just did that to produce the desired effect.

We didn't get along very well. He was always a half second ahead of me. If I flew a landing and ballooned, I knew I should apply power, but before I could, the throttle would fly out of my hand and I would get a load in my ears through the Gossports.

After eleven hours I still hadn't soloed. My shipmate had done it in eight. I was very discouraged and decided to quit. I guessed I didn't have the "right stuff." I informed my buddy of my decision and explained what the problem was. He said "bullshit" and volunteered to go up with me. He said he would get into the back seat and not touch the controls unless death was positively inevitable. I figured what the heck, he had soloed, and he had thirteen hours in his logbook. He was my "role model"; I wanted to be like him someday. We went out to the airport and climbed into the plane. I made three of the best takeoffs and landings I had ever made in my life.

With my confidence restored, the next time I got together with my instructor I explained the situation and asked if he would please give me one more second of time before he grabbed the controls? It wasn't too many more flights after that when we landed one day and taxied back to the fuel pumps. I was ready to shut down when he told me to "hold it." He got out of the back seat and before closing the door he picked up the speaking funnel and said, "Well, take it around, if you don't do any worse than you have been doing you probably won't kill yourself." With these words of encouragement ringing in my ears I soloed. I continued to build time in my logbook and things were going fine.

My sub was sent to Japan for six months and when I got back I found out that while I was gone the engine in the plane ate a valve and parts were being shipped out from stateside for repairs. I had been making steady progress towards my ticket but now things were at a standstill. The days turned into weeks and the weeks turned into months. When the ship was finally repaired I had so little time left before my discharge that I never got enough time in to get my license. My logbook showed about 34 hours before I left Hawaii.

After I got out of the Navy I went to college, got married, started my career, etc., etc. It's an old story and I am sure it has happened to more than one aspiring pilot. The years went by and I never touched a stick. The only things I flew were model airplanes, which I enjoyed very much and still do today. I never gave much thought to flying.

It seems strange to think of those days now. I find it hard to believe I actually flew an old 65 H.P. Interstate Cadet out of Honolulu International airport as a student. I wonder if you could do that today?

We did have a radio at least, such as it was. There was a switch on the instrument panel marked "on" and "off." One day I asked the instructor how I could tell if the radio was working? He told me, "Look under the seat, that's where the radio is, if you see the tubes glowing the damn thing is on."

In those days there was only one commercial flight a day from stateside. I wonder how many there are today? I came through there a couple of years back, I didn't recognize the place. I guess what they say is true, you can never go back.

THE CESSPOOL 150/150

One of the tow ships we had at the field was a Cessna 150 with a 150 H.P. engine and a prop pitched for climb. As a tow ship it was an absolute dog. It took forever to tow to two thousand feet behind this thing. In fact sometimes it never got there.

Cessna 150-150

On a hot, humid, midwest August day I was unfortunate enough to draw this ship for a tow. My demo passenger was a lady of ample proportions. As we rumbled down the runway towards the seven-foot corn at the upwind end of the field, I kept my hand on the tow release knob. I really didn't think we would make it. Finally the tow plane lifted off but only to about six feet. It drug its wheels through the corn tassels for what seemed like a mile. Slowly it climbed out of the corn and we cleared the telephone wires by about ten feet.

On and on we went inching our way skyward. After what seemed to be about a half an hour I glanced at the altimeter and saw 1900 feet. Great! I thought, only 100 feet to go and I can get off tow. A little while later I looked again and was surprised to see 1700. Back at 1800 again the tow pilot was rocking his wings vigorously. This is the universally adopted signal for the glider to release. I knew what was happening, all his gauges were redlining and in about one minute we would both become gliders when his engine blew up. Not good!

I released and made a normal demo flight from that point on. My lady passenger thought it was a great flight and said she thought it was a lot longer than she expected. Me too!

This ship was not only used for towing but was used for power instruction also. When I decided to get my power ticket, this was the plane I took my instruction in. I became well acquainted with the "Cesspool 150/150.

Mice loved this ship; they seemed to prefer it to all other aircraft at the field. They would crawl into the ship and build nests everywhere. Field mice don't have good potty manners. If they have to go to the bathroom they don't have the common decency to go outside to do it, they just do it anywhere. Thus the nickname "Cesspool 150/150."

If you had some flight time scheduled in that thing on a hot summer day, you had better get to the airport an hour early to prop the doors open and air it out before you had to fly. Even then it would just barely be tolerable. I used to wear earplugs when I flew it and a lot of times I considered sticking the plugs in my nose and to hell with my ears.

Not only did the Cesspool smell terrible, it also flew terrible. There was no such thing as hands off straight and level flight in that thing. If you let go of the yoke you would find yourself in an ever-tightening spiral to the left. I once did my long cross-country flight, which consisted of three legs and took the better part of an entire day in it. When I landed I had an Excedrin headache number one.

One winter when all the aircraft were being repaired for the coming soaring season, the "Cesspool" was completely refurbished. It was repainted and the inside was cleaned up. It looked like a new plane and it smelled a whole lot better too. Shortly after that a twister came through the airport one night and rolled it up into a ball. I disliked that plane but I hated to see it go.

DUTCH

Dutch was a real piece of work. When I decided to take up power flying the second time, he was my instructor in the "Cesspool 150/150." He wasn't anything like my first power instructor. Dutch was laid back, real cool, I never saw him get excited. Of course I wasn't anything like that cocky young kid who was learning to fly in Hawaii. Maybe that had something to do with it.

He was a little older than I was. He had fought in WWII and received the "Purple Heart." He never told me this but someone else did. If Dutch liked you he would teach you to fly for nothing but if he didn't like you, no amount of money would get him to fly with you. I guess he liked me.

"So what do I owe you?" I would ask after the lesson, while he was signing my logbook. "Aw hell," he would say, "just buy me a chicken dinner and we will have a few beers." Great! I thought. I soon learned this arrangement had its drawbacks. It damn near killed me.

All my instruction took place in the evening after work. I left the office about five and by the time I got to the airport it was after six. Dutch would finish up with his last glider student and by the time we untied the plane and did a pre-flight it was seven. We would fly till about 8:30, then top off the tanks, tie the ship down, de-brief, fill out the logbook and it was nine or a little later.

The chicken place was two towns west of the airport, about thirteen miles. The first pitcher of beer was gone by the time our chicken arrived so we would order another one. After the meal we would sit around and do some hanger flying while enjoying another pitcher of beer.

Sometime after eleven o'clock we would slosh out of the place and start the long drive home. It wasn't that I minded getting home after midnight so much, it was getting up at 4:45 in the morning that I minded. Dutch was a professional photographer and didn't have to get up till about eleven. Thank God I only did this a couple of nights a week. I think every night would have killed me.

One night as we worked on our after dinner pitcher, I told Dutch how I hated the hour and a half drive home. "Hell, it doesn't take me that long," he said with a wink and a sly grin. We got into our cars and left. His car was pointed in the right direction but mine wasn't. By the time I drove around the block and started off on course Dutch was nowhere in sight.

Approaching the next town I noticed a police car by the side of the road with its lights flashing. As I got nearer I saw Dutch's car parked ahead of the cruiser. I contemplated laying on the horn and giving him the royal salute but thought better of it. Heck, he was my instructor after all.

The "P" FACTOR

"P-factor" as it relates to powered aircraft is an aerodynamic force exerted on an airplane by the angle of the relative wind as it strikes the spinning propeller disk. "P" factor as it relates to a glider is something altogether different.

Glider pilots often spend the better part of a day flying about in a supine seated position, in a cramped cockpit, under a full-length canopy with the sun beating down on them. Dehydration is one of the glider pilot's worst enemies and more than one glider pilot has been killed by it. For this reason all those who fly gliders for long periods of time must carry enough drinking water with them to last the entire flight. "What goes up must come down" definitely applies to a glider and "what goes in must come out," definitely applies to a glider pilot.

Some of my glider flights were getting pretty long. While none of them were actually terminated by Mother Nature's call, her call was soon answered after I landed. I was planning on some even longer flights and so I thought I had better look into a solution to the expected problem.

I went down to the end of the field where the high performance ships were kept to seek some advice. Rudy was one of the more experienced pilots who has spent many long hours and covered some long distances in a glider so I thought I would ask him. Rudy told me that what I needed was an "external catheter" and that I could obtain one of these at a medical supply store.

The "external catheter" is a device consisting of a short condom attached to a long plastic tube. The other end of the tube can be inserted into a bottle, a plastic bag, or you can drill a hole in the bottom of your fuselage and let it dangle out there. I wondered what the EPA would think of the last option? I doubt that it would have any adverse effect on the crops below. You certainly wouldn't want to use it in a thermal with your friends circling close below. Common decency would prohibit its use when flying low over outdoor assemblies like picnics, baseball games or family reunions.

So off to the medical supply store I went. As luck would have it there didn't seem to be anything but female help in the place. I looked around for awhile and soon a lady said, "Could I help you sir?" I explained what I wanted and she led me to a shelf where they were on display. It was obvious I had never purchased one of these things before so she asked, "What size is the fixture sir?" I replied, "Say what?" "What size is the fixture sir, I assume it is for you?" At first I thought I would just tell her that I never had any complaints but it seemed to me she wanted a more definitive answer. It soon became apparent that I had no idea what size my fixture was. Then the lady handed me a cardboard gauge and said, "Here, take this home with you and measure yourself and then come back and we will see that you get a proper fit." I grabbed the gauge, thanked the lady, and hurried out of the store.

Outside in the car I examined the thing. My God! Up until that very moment I was pretty well satisfied with my fixture, not anymore. After four years in the Navy I thought I was pretty knowledgeable about the male anatomy, apparently not. Any guy that would measure in the upper twenty five percent of this gauge should be careful. If he drops his drawers in the barn he will scare the hell out of the cows. My wife wanted to know what was going on and when I showed her the gauge she giggled all the way home.

I never went back to that store. I figured the lady would say, "Oh, well sir, that would be over here in the boys department."

DORT

I believe every man or woman born is allotted a certain amount of good luck in their lifetime. I also believe I spent most of mine in one fell swoop on the day I married Doris, nicknamed Dort. Throughout a lifetime of aviation interests she was always by my side. An understanding wife is the greatest asset a "propellerhead" like me can have.

Dort

When I first started flying gliders she would accompany me to the glider field every weekend. After I became a demo pilot and then an instructor she was always there. She became in effect the "Airport Mother."

We would get up early Saturday morning and head for the field some fifty miles away. Sometimes we would stop along the way for breakfast. By nine o'clock we were there and my day began. I was busy with passengers and students and Dort was busy watching other pilot's children and dogs. She enjoyed talking to the other wives. Everyone knew her and liked her. She became famous for her chocolate chip cookies.

Around noon I would join her again to wolf down a lunch she had packed and then I would go back to work again. We really didn't see all that much of each other during the day. Sometimes it would be dark by the time my day ended. We would head out to a small restaurant for dinner and then start off on the long drive home. Sunday would be the same thing all over again. She seemed to enjoy it and I never heard her complain.

It sometimes amazed me the things aeronautical she picked up just hanging out with me. Once on the Ohio toll road on our annual trip to our hometown, she remarked that we ought to be getting pretty good gas mileage. "Why?' I asked, "because we have a tail wind," she said. I looked at a flag and she was right. Dort was forever looking at clouds and commenting on soaring conditions.

I do a lot of engine testing in my driveway. Trying out a new propeller or tweaking a carburetor. After one such test I went into the kitchen to get a drink of water. "That didn't sound right to me," she said. She was right, I was shooting for 5000-RPM static and I was only getting 4500. Five hundred off and she caught it, not bad.

It no longer surprises her to find an engine crankcase in the oven and a set of crankshaft bearings in the freezer section of her refrigerator. She got good at distinguishing between the smell of drying butyrate dope, curing polyester resin or hot cutting oil. She never said much about the two eight foot outboard wing panels sitting in the guest bedroom for over a year and a half. In case you are getting the wrong idea, she is a meticulous housekeeper.

She was there the day I bailed out; she saw the whole thing. I drifted down under a blue and white canopy and landed in a bean field. She was the first to reach me as I stood there with my arms full of used parachute. She didn't kiss me or hug me or even say anything, she just stood there in wide-eyed amazement. I think she was a little out of it. Never once did she suggest that I might consider another hobby.

After forty some years of marriage she is still with me. I like to think I am a fairly good husband. I know I will never be as good at it as she is at being a wife.

On the day we said "I do," I got the best of the deal. If she should die before I do, I think the Blessed Virgin Mary will come down and personally escort her up to heaven. The church will probably make her a saint. Someday I may see her smiling down from a stained glass window at me, probably holding a part of an airplane.

WILBUR

Wilbur was one of those people you meet now and then that seem to have a way of sticking in your mind. I didn't see him all that much but still he stuck.

The sun was just peeking over the horizon as I went rolling down the runway heading straight for it. A little backpressure on the stick and the Mitchell B-10 ultralight flying wing lifted off. God, how I love these early morning flights! The sun is low, the shadows are long and everything is so fresh, clean and peaceful. The early morning flights and those I make just as the sun is setting are the ones I enjoy the most.

It was early autumn and the fields below were a multitude of greens and browns. The tops of some trees were just beginning to show some color. My thick sweater, leather jacket, gloves and boots offered adequate protection but I still knew it was cool and I knew winter was not far off. Flying out in the open like this may shorten the season somewhat but I wouldn't trade it for anything. An enclosure of any kind makes it a whole different ball game. When I fly through a little wisp of cloud I not only see it, I feel it, and I taste it.

So there I was at 1000 feet and one mile north of the town of Hinckley, just drinking it in. Strange how fast things change! The whole airframe began to shake violently and the old "Mac 101" go-cart engine made a noise like it was eating itself.

For about 1.5 seconds I thought about making it back to the field and I fed in the control inputs for a left turn. The vibrations were so bad, I thought the engine would tear itself of the motor mounts. I hit the kill switch and put the thing out of its misery.

The left turn revealed a small rather long triangular piece of what looked like pasture, everything else was eight foot tall corn. Now,

Mitchel B-10

I know what they say about pasture and how it should be your absolutely last choice for an emergency landing but to me it looked like the only choice, besides it did look fairly smooth. The field had corn on one side, a creek, bushes and trees on other and a gravel road along the end. At least it was lined up with the wind and the approach end was clear of wires and other hazards.

The landing was pretty bumpy and I used my brake to stop. Brake! What a joke, it consisted of a ¾ inch square piece of 4130 steel with a bicycle grip on one end, the other end just scrapes on the ground. This is the same setup I used to use on those cars I built out of orange crates when I was 10 years old. Seems I haven't made much progress. Anyhow, after plowing a furrow any farmer would have been proud of, I came to a stop with room to spare.

After a quick check showed no damage to plane or pilot, I undid my seat belts and walked around behind the engine. I moved the prop about four inches and the sound it made was disgusting, that engine would require lots of work. Later that week when I tore it down, I found out just how much work. The cages of the wrist pin bearings had failed and the needle bearings had escaped. Strange things happen when a couple dozen needles start flying around inside an engine turning over seven thousand RPM. The piston looked like a porcupine with all those needles stuck on end in the piston top. They were everywhere. I even found some in the carburetor.

The Mac 101 was a twelve-pound engine that put out twelve H.P. at 11000 R.P.M.; it wasn't built for longevity. The people at the go-cart shop got to know me pretty well. It was funny, but every time that I went there I would be forced to act out this little charade with the owner. It went like this: "What are these parts for?" "A go-cart." "Well, okay, but if these parts were to be used for an ultralight I couldn't sell them to you." " They are for a go-cart." "Well, okay." He knew I was lying and I knew he knew I was lying. Still, every time it was the same thing all over again. Maybe it wasn't all that funny, after awhile I got tired of it but if I wanted the parts----.

I pushed the B-10 to the edge of the pasture and stuck its nose into the corn to protect it as much as possible from the wind. There was a farmhouse nearby but I decided not to go pounding on any doors that early in the morning. This was a workday for me as a flight instructor at Hinckley Soaring and I had to be there at ten o'clock that morning. There were a lot of things to do and I didn't have much time to do them.

In 1973 I went out to Hinckley Soaring just to take a ride. Oh yeah, right! That was 27 years ago and I am still hanging around out there. I went from private pilot, to commercial pilot, to flight instructor. Anyhow I had to work and I probably wouldn't be able to retrieve the ship until sometime later that evening and I would need some help.

Grabbing my chute, I climbed the embankment to the gravel road, walked down that to the two-lane blacktop heading into town and began to hitchhike. The first person to come along was a young man in a pickup truck who stopped with a rather surprised look on his face. I guess my helmet, goggles and parachute were a tip-off that I wasn't your average hitchhiker. I told him my story and asked him if he could take me out to the airport? He said he couldn't do that as he was already late for work but he would drop me off on the square of Hinckley and I could try my luck there.

For some reason my costume didn't work as well on the square in Hinckley and after a while I gave up hitchhiking. Hinckley is a Midwest farm town of 1600 and it has a combination bakery/restaurant that opens at 5:00 AM for the farmers to enjoy their first cup. I thought that maybe I could find a ride there.

As I stepped through the door, twenty heads swiveled on twenty necks and forty eyes opened wide. I felt like I was a cat looking at a tree full of owls. When they were sure I wasn't an alien from the planet "Dacron" they went back to drinking coffee and I made my big announcement; "Is anyone here going out towards the airport?" Silence. Then after what seemed to be an eternity, a very, very old man at the end of the counter said in a quivery voice, "If you will wait till I finish my coffee, I'll take you out there." Excellent! I thought.

I plopped down on the stool next to him, introduced myself and ordered a cup. He said his name was Wilbur and yes he used to be a pilot too, a long time ago when I was but a babe in my mothers' arms. "She was a Waco," he said, "red one, purty airplane." Then he proceeded to do some pretty fancy hangar flying. I was getting a kick out of him. Wilbur started flying back in the early thirties. He took his dual in an Aero Marine Klemm, a German designed, low wing, open cockpit monoplane.

The airport he flew from is no longer there; it is now a bean field. In those days it was known as "DeKalb County Airport" and it was an airmail field. If Chicago was socked in, they would put out railroad flares in a certain pattern and the pilots would land there.

The mail would then be sent on to Chicago by train. Somewhere about 1936, Wilbur and another fellow became partners in an OX-5 powered Waco, "a red one, purty airplane." The love of his life it seems.

I was really enjoying the conversation with the old guy but soon our coffee was gone. Wilbur picked up his cane and shuffled out the door towards his car at the curb in front and I collected my gear and followed along. We were stuffing my junk into the trunk when another patron who followed us out, motioned me aside. "If you are going to ride with Wilbur, you might want to wear that helmet of yours," he said. Oh fine! I thought, I survived an emergency landing only to die with Wilbur behind the wheel.

It was a straight three-mile shot to the airport, good road, no intersections, little traffic, what could go wrong? We started out and I gave Wilbur my undivided attention. He drove fine, a little slow perhaps, but what the heck. We got to the airport safely and I got out, thanked him and said goodbye.

The trailer was unhitched from my car and I drove back to the farm where I had landed. I pulled into the lane and cautiously got out.

Most farmers have dogs and most farm dogs think they own the whole damn farm and that includes the road that passes by it. No dog, lucky for me.

A few raps at the door and the farmer answered. I told him I had made an emergency landing in his field. "Oh yeah, I saw you." Can you believe that, 6:30 AM, no engine and the guy saw me? Would it be okay to leave it there until this evening? "Sure." I asked him if it would it be safe there? "Well, lots of kids play by the creek, I don't know?" Great! Well, I'd have to take my chances.

There was still time for breakfast before work so I headed back to the bakery. When I got there everyone made a big fuss over me. "What you still alive?" "We thought we would never see you again." I told them I didn't know what they were talking about and that Wilbur never exceeded 45. "That's right" they said, "He doesn't and he doesn't stop for stop signs, traffic lights or other traffic either." Lucky me!

With breakfast over, I headed for the field and the workday began. It was a good day for thermals. Every time I hooked into a boomer with a student or a demo, I would fly out over the farm and check on the Mitchell. Everything looked fine. This was a rather foolish thing to do. What was I going to do if I did see someone messing around, strafe them? Still I was concerned, that was my pride and joy sitting down there. It took me three years to glue all those little pieces together, a lot of blood; sweat and tears went into that thing. I was concerned.

Finally the day ended and I tied the last glider down. Two of my friends volunteered to help me disassemble the ship and put it into the trailer. We drove out to the farm and pulled the car and trailer in as close as we could on the gravel road. The wing was folded and detached from the hang cage and all the parts were carried to the trailer. In about one hour I was ready for the long drive home.

My wife and I moved to Hinckley several years ago and Wilbur is no longer with us. For the first few years he was and occasionally I would meet him here and there. It was always the same thing, "Hi Wilbur, how you doing? "Hi," he would say and then he would squint and say, "Who the hell are you?" I would tell him I was the pilot he met at the bakery and drove out to the airport. He would think awhile and then say, "Oh yeah, say did I ever tell you I used to fly, she was a Waco, red one, purty airplane---."

SPIN OFFS

It seems to me it doesn't matter what hobby or sport you become interested in, sooner or later you will get interested in other things that pertain to that hobby or sport.

When I first began to fly gliders I would take a logbook and a pen to the field with me. Nowadays, I show up with an airline captains flight case and an additional attaché case in my car and both are full of stuff I just can't live without.

Is there a pilot alive who hasn't become an amateur meteorologist? Glider pilots in particular are very interested in weather. Soaring is a solar powered sport. The sun is the engine that drives the earth's weather and soaring is very weather related.

I have lots of books on the subject of weather. A weather report on TV or the radio is of great importance to me and all other soaring pilots. We used to have a TV weatherman on one station in Chicago who was more of a clown than a weatherman. Although the average viewer probably got a kick out of this guy, I hated him. I used to fantasize about performing a service to the soaring community with my 222-varmint rifle and a nine-power scope.

When I first learned to use thermals to stay up in a glider for a while, I found out that soaring birds make excellent thermal markers. If I saw a bird making lazy circles in the sky I would head that direction and sure enough I would be rewarded with some good lift. If the bird was flapping its wings and heading in a straight line I would ignore it. I knew it was looking for a thermal just like me.

It soon became apparent that not all these birds looked alike and so I became a bird watcher or "birder" as they are referred to. I bought a book on birds and a new hobby was born. I soon found out that most of the soaring birds I saw were hawks, "Red Tails" mostly but there were other varieties. Occasionally I would spot a "Turkey Vulture" commonly referred to as a Buzzard and on rare occasions an Eagle.

One day a student of mine landed and was very excited. He said he was in a thermal with at least one hundred hawks. I figured he was just exaggerating. Then one day as I banked the glider steeply in a thermal I looked down the wing and saw it. It was as though I was looking down a hawk lined funnel and yes, there must have been a hundred of them. I never saw that again but on that day I did.

When I used to see a bush full of small birds I would just assume they were sparrows. Now I see many different birds in that bush. I now know that there are about twenty-six different types of sparrows on the eastside of the Rocky Mountains alone. Bird watching has become an interesting pastime for me. Just like the weather, I probably would not have become very interested in it if I hadn't gotten into soaring in the first place.

Funny the spin offs you can get into when you are pursuing just one other hobby or sport.

LIFT IS WHERE YOU FIND IT

It is impossible to remember every flight I have ever made and it is impossible to forget some of them.

The irritating sound of the alarm clock woke me from a sound sleep and I let it run its course rather than make the effort to turn it off. Fumbling around on the nightstand I found the weather radio and turned it on to the preset N.O.A.A. station. A voice that was strangely reminiscent of Count Dracula gave the weather forecast. I cannot place this guys' accent; I would say Transylvania. The current conditions were: temperature, 44 degrees, humidity, 75 percent, and winds calm. Perfect! I pulled the bedroom drapes open to confirm what I had heard and was greeted with a clear black sky and brightly shinning stars. Not a leaf was stirring.

After throwing my clothes on I headed for the bathroom and splashed some water on my face to bring myself fully awake. In the kitchen I heated two cups of yesterday's coffee in the microwave, poured it into my insulated mug and got into my Jeep.

It was dark, forget predawn, it was still night. "Jacks'" Amoco station was open even at that early hour so I pulled in to get something to go with my coffee. A cream filled Long John with maple icing beckoned to me from the smudged glass case. I grabbed it. Paid for it. And jumped back into the Jeep and headed west. A long line of headlights was heading east into the city, guys going to work, poor devils.

My "Moni" motor-glider is based at "Wade" airport eight miles away and that is where I was headed. A rusty "T" hanger and 3000 feet of rolling sod runway is all there is but it is heaven to me. In the spring a small stream runs across the south end of the runway about 600 feet in from the threshold making it unusable. Occasionally I have seen deer or fox on the runway. This summer the owner shot a raccoon in the office. I guess you could say it is quaint.

Moni Motorglider

The 100-watt bulb high up in the rafters didn't provide much light but it was just enough to see. I undid the down locks on the hanger door and took a strain on the chain hoist. The door creaked and moaned and began to rise, thirty-four pulls and it was fully open. Even with the door open there was little light out there to help. The preflight was done with the aid of a flashlight. Before I untied the ship I ran the engine up; no use untying the thing if it wasn't going to start. The ship was untied and pulled outside.

You don't get in a "Moni," you put it on. I once met a man who was selling one because he could no longer fit in it. Three hundred and fourteen pounds of aluminum doesn't buy a whole lot of interior space.

My leather jacket and my chute made even me at 155 pounds feel wall to wall. The seating position is rather supine with your knees about level with your shoulders. The Moni has a single main wheel with a tail wheel and wheels at the end of the wing tips. This further exaggerates the laid back feeling. Visibility forward while taxiing is nonexistent.

I snubbed the five point safety belts down, strapped my hand-held radio to my leg, attached the antenna to the radio and adjusted the altimeter. After getting all comfy I punched the starter and the stopwatch and was ready to go. The condensation had formed on the inside of my canopy so I took a rag and cleaned off a patch on both sides. At least I would be able to see the sides of the runway. I felt a little like Charles Lindbergh, only being able to see out the sides.

"Wade traffic, Experimental 48 Mike Golf departing runway 18, Wade." I wondered if any other fool was up to hear me? Once upon a time I got fooled however and I will never do that again. It was 6:27 AM. I got a thing about early morning flights.
It was still pretty dark out and the tinted bubble canopy did nothing to help. In the dim light I pushed the throttle forward till it hit the stop and watched the needles of the instruments climb. None of then touched the little red lines on their faces so everything was cool.

The ailerons became effective first and I leveled the wings. The tail came up at about 40. Forward pressure on the stick kept me glued to the runway till I saw 60 on the airspeed and then a little back pressure got me up and away.

At 200 feet I turned right and noticed the tops of the predicted front glowing pink far off to the west; they must have been thirty to fifty thousand feet high. The streetlights were still on in the town of Waterman, and a steady stream of headlights was heading west. I stayed close to the field till I had 1250' on the altimeter and then headed for Lake Shabbona to check out the fisherman. They weren't up yet.

The airport in DeKalb has a new runway and I decided to give it a try, I certainly wouldn't have to worry about traffic. I called my intentions on the radio and entered a left downwind for runway 20. That new runway is 5001'X 100' and the center line is wider than my fuselage. I never landed on such a big thing before. I turned right at the first ramp and then right again to back taxi parallel to the runway.

Much to my surprise a Beechcraft Baron was on the taxi-way ahead of me and was just turning right on a ramp leading to the runway. The baron stopped and just stood there and stood there. I was just about to mash the mike button and ask what their intentions were when I figured it out. I think they were looking at me, I could just imagine the conversation, "What the hell is that?" After regaining the runway, I took off again and just flew around here and there. The fields below were a patchwork of gold and russets, fall was coming, and it was beautiful. My fuel was down to about half so I decided to head for home.

As I flew towards Wade I noticed the front was getting closer and now there was a long thin cloud in front of the front itself.

This cloud stretched for miles in a southwest-northeast direction. My "Moni" normally climbs at 300 FPM but as I approached the long thin cloud my vario began to register 500 to 700. Climbing over the cloud at about 2500' AGL I got strong sink on the backside. Making a 180 I climbed back over the top and began to play in the lift. Shutting the engine off I pulled the nose up to 55 MPH and stopped the windmilling prop.

Back and forth I soared along that cloud. I wasn't going up but I wasn't going down either. I was having a ball. It was 7:25 in the morning and I was soaring! The thought occurred to me that I might be the first person to soar over Hinckley, Illinois at that time of day. Soon I noticed I was drifting east at a pretty good clip and I began to feel a little uncomfortable. The mag and the master were switched on, the choke pulled out half way and the throttle was cracked. I punched the start button and the engine sprang to life. Well it didn't exactly spring, it more or less staggered, but it did run.

Climbing up over the cloud again I headed for Wade. I didn't head far before the ground started to disappear and I realized I was getting into the front. Making a 180 I dove back over the cloud and made another 180 and flew under it. Once below the cloud I could see the base of the front was slopping down towards the ground at a rather steep angle. It looked like it would be a race to see if I made it to Wade before the cloud did. If it really got bad I could always land at Hinckley airport, that was my way out. I pushed the stick forward to get 95MPH and headed straight for the field. I won, but not by much.

The ship was pushed back into the hanger, the tank was topped off and I filled out my logbook. It was still early so I decided to look for mushrooms along the edge of the runway. Jumping into the Jeep I drove the full length of the field on both sides, stopping now and then to pick a few. It began to rain but I didn't care. By the time I did both sides I was pretty wet but I had quite a lot of mushrooms.

What a great day! I had a nice "Dawn Patrol," did some soaring and picked a nice mess of mushrooms, and it still wasn't nine o'clock.

Forest Gump said: "Life is like a box of chocolates, you never know what you will get." I guess lift is a lot like a mushroom, you never know where you will find it, or when for that matter.

STINKY DOG

One of my students was a young girl who was a senior in high school. She was a good pilot but she had a little trouble with book learning. Looking at her logbook I realized that she had flown more types of gliders in more different places than I had. She just had trouble studying the books.

Some people can take a stack of books and a test guide, study them and after awhile go take the test and pass it. Other people do better in a classroom type of environment. Still others seem to need a lot of personal tutoring. This gal fell into the later category. I spent an awful lot of time tutoring her.

Her mother was a private pilot and her father was an airline pilot. Sometimes the mother would fly her daughter out to the field to take her glider lessons in the family Cessna 140. This ship was one of the most beautiful Cessna 140s I had ever seen.

It was polished aluminum with red trim. I don't know if it was ever entered in competition at "Oshkosh" or not but I am sure it would have won if it had been. I couldn't help wondering how many buckets of metal polish and elbow grease went into getting it that way. It was a "10" both inside and out.

One Saturday the mother and daughter arrived in this beautiful ship accompanied by their little "French Poodle." The dog was beautiful too. It was snow white and had a little red bow on its head. Its toenails were painted to match the bow in its hair. It was adorable I suppose, if you like that sort of dog. I'm more of a "Black Lab" type of guy myself.

Everyone was sitting on the porch of the office/trailer and they were all petting it and scratching its ears. The dog loved it and was scampering back and forth in and out of the office greeting each new arrival and receiving more attention, petting and scratching.

After awhile it apparently grew bored with all this adulation and ran down under the porch deck. There it discovered a gap in the ground skirt around the base of the trailer. The dog went in there and in the gloom of the half-light it met a new friend.

This new friend was all black with a white stripe running from its head to the tip of its tail. The new friend introduced itself.

Those on the porch had more or less forgotten about the dog but were reminded of its whereabouts by a most horrible yelping. The little poodle came tearing out from under the porch. It threw itself on the ground and proceeded to roll about as though it was in some terrible pain. Then it drug its behind for about five yards in the grass all the while yelping like crazy.

The mother and daughter leapt off the porch and began chasing the poodle about until they succeeded in capturing it. From the look on their faces I am not so sure they were happy with their success. Some one went into town and purchased a large can of tomato juice and the dog was given a bath in it. I saw recently on TV that all that does is make the dog smell like a tomato for a while and then it starts to smell like a rancid tomato and then it reverts to smelling like a skunk. The poor poodle was repeatedly hosed off with the garden hose, and then it was sprayed with canopy cleaner and hosed off some more. As the sun sank slowly in the west it was put into the plane and the three passengers took off for home.

I couldn't believe they put that stinking dog in that beautiful airplane. I understand their not wanting to leave it behind although I don't believe any harm would have come to it. No other creature would come closer than twenty feet to it.

I thought they would be better off to have obtained some used tow line and lashed it to the outboard end of the wing strut or to the lower end of the landing gear leg. A half-hour ride in a ninety-mile an hour slipstream might have blown some of the stink off.

I wonder if they had to replace the interior of that beautiful airplane?

BROWN EYES

It was a weekend at the soaring field and the place was jumping, even though it was still early in the morning. I was flying demos and doing instruction.

They gave her to me for a demo. She must have been eight or nine years old and cute as a bug's ear in her little flowered dress. Most little girls don't come out to the airport to take a glider ride wearing a dress. In fact most big girls don't either.

I asked her how much she weighed and when she told me, I knew we were going to need lots of ballast. Grabbing a ballast bar for the glider and a big bag of lead shot I figured that would do the job.

I handed her a couple of cushions and a big slab of four-inch foam rubber I carry with me for just such occasions. I don't like to see someone give a demo flight to a little kid when they can't even see out of the cockpit.

Funny, I can't remember any adults with her but I am sure she didn't drive out to the airport alone. Usually the parents follow along for the loading. There is a lot of smiling and talking and then of course it is a great photo op. I just can't remember anyone being there.

We headed down the line to the glider. I told her to be careful of the wing as I pulled the ship out onto the runway and swung it around into the wind. After installing the ballast bar in its holder and putting the bag of shot under the seat cushion I put the other cushions and the foam in place. Lifting her up I got her seated and belted in.

All the while we are doing this I was trying to carry on a conversation. I was a dismal failure. What does one say to a little eight-year-old girl in a pretty flowered dress?

The tow plane arrived and I ran the towline back to the ship and attached it to the tow hook on the belly of the glider. I told her that I would close and lock the canopy and get into the seat behind her. It was then that her little hand rested on my arm, "Mister" she said, I looked down into the biggest, and prettiest, brownest eyes I had ever seem. "Yes?," I said. "Promise me you won't fly upside down." I promised.

We were off. She became a little more talkative during the flight. I pointed out this and that to her and she seemed to be enjoying the whole thing. The flight wasn't a long one but maybe it was just long enough for her.

When we landed there was another demo ride waiting at the end of the field and I hurried to unload her. Our parting was brief. She said it was "fun" and she thanked me. I watched her walk away carrying all those pillows and foam.

I wondered what this brief encounter with aviation would mean to her? Did it cause a spark that would become a small fire and would that small fire then become a blaze? Would she someday pilot an airliner between Chicago and some far distant city? It could happen. It has happened before.

GOOD IN VEGETABLE SOUP

The Mitchell B-10 was the first homebuilt airplane that I constructed. It was an ultralight flying wing and was powered by a 12 HP go-cart engine. I loved it. What a joy it was to float around over the cornfields at 400 feet and 35 miles per hour.

Most of the time I had it I would haul it out to the airfield in its trailer, assemble it and fly. When it wasn't flying, the wing was folded up in the trailer. We were living in a townhouse at the time and since ours was an end unit we had a small fenced in side yard. The trailer sat in this yard under a big beautiful Maple tree.

One day when I was working on the trailer I noticed some seed like objects scattered about on top of the trailer. They were not like anything I had ever seen drop out of a maple tree before and I know maple trees. These things were cylindrical in shape, about three eighths of an inch long and about three-sixteenths inch in diameter.

I couldn't figure out what they were so I gathered some up and put them into a tiny jar with a screw cap on it. I took them to the office and showed them around to everybody. No one could figure them out. No one knew what they were. I crumbled one up between my thumb and finger and dabbed some of the powder on my tongue. It tasted rather peppery and it reminded me of a seasoning my father used to put into homemade vegetable soup. The name of that spice as I recall was "Summer Savory" and it really enhanced the flavor of soup. I popped a whole one in my mouth and it was good.

I was determined to find out what these things were. Then I remembered someone who maybe could help me. When I lived in the old neighborhood in Chicago, there was a guy who lived across the alley who worked for the River Forrest Forestry Department. His name was Nick. I gave Nick a call on the phone and told him of my discovery and he was puzzled. Nick told me to put the jar on my back porch and he would drop by and see if he could identify them.

The next morning I put the jar on the porch before I went to work. When I got home that night it was still there. Days went by and I didn't hear from Nick. I was beginning to think he forgot to even come by and look at the things.

Then one day as I was walking along the street in my natty little three piece business suit and power tie, to catch the 7:05 to the office, we met.

It was pretty crowded, everybody going to work. I noticed a nice looking young lady up ahead and as I passed her I gave her a nice smile and said, "Good morning." She smiled and returned the greeting. I heard a horn blowing and there was Nick parked on the other side of the street in a forestry department truck. He rolled down the window and yelled at the top of his lungs. "Hey Ron, ya know dat stuff dats been fallin out of yer tree, dat stuff ya been eatin, it's Squirrel Shit."

The nice looking young lady behind me giggled.

A REAL AIRPLANE

Rudy figured he would kill two birds with one stone. Not only would he fly a 500-kilometer task (320 miles), he would fly a little farther and set a new Illinois State record for the longest triangular course flown.

He filled out his declaration, had it witnessed and meticulously readied his ship and himself for the task. It was a good day and he was off on his quest as the first thermals of the day started to pop.

He rounded his turn point of the first leg of the triangular course, banked the ship up on a wing tip and fired his cameras. The cameras would take a picture of his wing pointing down at some recognizable landmark, a highway intersection, a railroad crossing a river, etc., etc. This photo would prove he had been there. Then he was off on course for the next turn point. It wasn't exactly a piece of cake. Sometimes he would get low and have to really search for a thermal to gain altitude and save the flight. Occasionally he had to go far off course to find the lift but he persevered.

At his third turn point he took his photo and now he was on his last leg. It was getting late in the day and the sun's rays were striking the ground at a lower angle. The land was beginning to cool off. The thermals were less frequent and not as strong as they had been earlier in the day. It soon became apparent to him that although he had the 500 K in the bag, he was not going to set a new state record. He had to find a place to land and he had to find it quick.

There was an airport just within gliding distance and he headed for it. It was a squeaker but he made it. The gliders wheel gently kissed the blacktop and the ship coasted to a stop. He hopped out and took off his chute. After pushing the ship out of harms way he began looking around the airport.

Rudy had lots of things to do. He had to find a witness to sign his declaration. He had to find a phone so he could make a call to his home field and get a tow plane fly out and tow him out of there. The sun was going down.

After walking around for awhile he found two guys working on a single engine power plane. They could be his witnesses. He talked to them briefly and they told him where he could find a phone.

The call was made and a tow plane was dispatched. When the tow plane landed, the glider was pushed out on the runway, the towrope hooked up and they were off. It was on the way back that Rudy remembered that he forgot to do one very important thing. He had forgotten to ask one of the men working on the power plane to sign as a witness to his landing.

The next day he called the airport he had been forced to land on and asked if anyone knew the name and address of one of the men working on the airplane that he had spoken to the evening before. As luck would have it someone did and they provided him with the information.

Rudy sent the declaration and a few bucks along with a short note. He asked the guy to sign his declaration and use the money to buy a couple of drinks for his trouble. Several days later he received an envelope from the power pilot. The declaration was signed, the money was returned and a short note informed Rudy to keep the money and use it for lessons in a real airplane.

This didn't make Rudy very happy. He had flown B-17s in WWII and he thought they were real airplanes. So he kept the money and sent along a little note saying, "the next time you fly your real airplane, climb up to 2000 feet and turn the engine off, then fly 320 miles."

THE DAY WE BURIED BILL

Well we didn't exactly bury him, like we didn't dig a hole and put him in it. We dumped him out of an airplane.

Right after WW II, Bill and his brother Earl came home from the service to live with their parents in the big house on Broad Street. Bill had his wife Colleen with him.

I must have been in the seventh grade about that time and I was in love with model airplanes. One night as I was walking down the ally I heard the unmistakable sound of a model airplane engine running. I peered into the window of a basement that was filled with blue smoke and I yelled something to attract attention. They invited me in and that's how I met Bill, Earl and their father who all built model airplanes.

This was the beginning of a long friendship with the entire family. You might say they sort of adopted me, at least in so far as model airplanes went. They taught me the skills necessary to build and fly a really good model airplane. They were perfectionists and they made me do some things over so often that I would sometimes get mad. I would swear I would have nothing further to do with them. This would sometimes last for three days and then I would be right back down in their basement again.

Many an early Sunday morning, Bill, Earl, their father, Colleen, and I would pile into their cars along with various assorted models and related paraphernalia and head off for some model contest somewhere in Ohio. One such contest was held in conjunction with the dedication ceremony of the opening of the Canton Akron airport. At that time I was flying a free flight model called a "Buccaneer "B" Special." An Olsen Rice "23" engine that I borrowed from my uncle powered it. On one flight as I prepared to launch the model, a photographer stepped forward and snapped my picture.

On Monday morning my photo along with others appeared on the front page of the "Canton Repository." The caption read, "Ronald Martelet of Louisville Ohio aims his Buccaneer for the blue while his ground crew waits expectantly. The model climbed 25 seconds under power and then headed off across country." Monday afternoon the phone rang and it was my uncle, he wanted his engine back.

So there I was with a nice flying model but no engine to power it. It would take a whole summer of mowing grass to accumulate that kind of money. I didn't have a whole summer left. I was really blue.

About a week later on a Tuesday evening I asked Bill and Earl if they were going to the monthly meeting of the model airplane club in Canton. They said they couldn't make it, so I hitch hiked the seven miles to Canton to attend the meeting by myself. In the middle of the meeting someone walked down the aisle and a brown paper covered package was handed down the row of seats to me. I asked what it was and where it came from and he said he didn't know what it was and that someone he didn't know delivered it to the door. I unwrapped the package and there was a brand new "Olsen 23." I never could get those guys to admit they bought me that engine.

When I got out of high school it was my turn to go to war, the Korean War. I joined the Navy and from then on I seldom got back to Louisville. Bill died and Earl moved away. Now and then I would see Colleen and we would shoot the breeze awhile, talk about old times.

About two years ago I was visiting Louisville. I had just come out of the supermarket and it was raining real hard. I sat down on a bench under an awning and lit a cigar. Funny, I began to think about giving Colleen a call when just then I saw her walking across the parking lot. We talked awhile and then she asked if I would do her a favor and asked if I would follow her out to her house. I figured she wanted me to move something heavy or fix something that needed repairing and I said I would.

When we got there, we had a drink and talked awhile, then she excused herself and went into the other room. She came back with a black box about the size of a loaf of bread. She explained that the box contained the remains of Bill. She said she had them around for a long time and couldn't think of a proper way to dispose of them. At one time she had considered taking them out west where they had met and dumping them in the Rio Grande River, then she said she remembered that Bill did not like Mexicans.

Since Bill was in the Air Force and loved to build and fly model airplanes she thought it might be appropriate to dump him from an airplane. This was the favor she asked of me. I told her that my ship was presently in pieces all over the garage floor but as soon as it was air worthy I would honor her request.

We hauled Bill back to Illinois. My wife had a thing about his remains and wouldn't let me bring him into the house. For months he sat on the corner of the workbench out in the garage and kept me company while I put my plane back together. I introduced him to anyone who dropped by to check on my progress.

One night my wife and I visited another couple to see their new home. My friend Rick was a pilot too and he had a Cessna 150, which he kept in pristine condition. We were sitting in the kitchen having cake and coffee when I thought I would kid Rick a little. I mentioned Bill and asked if he might let me perform the aerial burial from his 150. Much to my surprise he became very enthusiastic and grabbed a piece of paper and began to make sketches of an ejection device.

The device he designed consisted of a three-foot long piece of five-inch diameter PVC plumbing pipe. It would have a flapper at one end held closed by a shock cord and the other end would have screw cap with a spring-loaded vent. Bill's remains would be loaded into the tube and the cap replaced. When we reached a nice spot the tube would be held out the window, the flapper released and the vent opened. Great!

On Thanksgiving Day 1996, Rick called me about nine A.M., and asked me if I wanted to do the job and I said, "OK." It was a beautiful day, the sun was shining, the sky was blue and about two inches of new snow covered the ground.

Rick picked Bill and me up and we drove to the airport. The Cessna was pulled out of the hanger and given a careful preflight. We loaded Bill into the device careful not to spill any of him and took off.

We flew south until we hit the Illinois River at Ottawa and turned west. It wasn't long till we came to a beautiful spot. Rick asked me to take the controls and he would handle the ejection. He opened the window and stuck the device out. He released the flapper, pushed the vent and there went Bill. Rick said it was beautiful. A long gray plume of ashes strung out behind us. Rick said anybody on the ground watching us would think we were on fire.

Mission accomplished, we headed back to the airport. As we were pushing the plane back into the hanger, Rick noticed that all the paint on the leading edge of the horizontal stabilizer had been blasted off. Rick wasn't too happy. Well, Bill always was sort of abrasive.

BE CONSIDERATE OF OTHER PEOPLE

I once had this crusty old flight instructor tell me the following: "Please try to be considerate of other people. If you are going to crash, crash on the airport, if not on the airport, then in some nice area as close to the airport as possible.

For God's sake don't drill it in some God forsaken mosquito infested woods and certainly not in a swamp.

A lot of people are going to be involved. The paramedics will have to come out to the crash scene. If you are dead the mortician will be involved. If the thing burns the fire department will come out. The National Transportation Safety Board will send a team out and the Federal Aviation Administration will be there too. Don't forget all the curious onlookers who will rush out there to see your dead ass.

Be considerate of other people. Crash on the airport. Try not to hit anything."

DROP IN ANYTIME

So there I was, fat dumb and happy. It was about seven in the morning; I was at 1250 feet above the ground and about 35 miles from my home field. It was a beautiful morning and I was drinking it all in when it happened. There was a deafening silence and I watched the prop of my "Moni" motor-glider spin down and stop horizontally. I could not believe my eyes or ears but it happened.

I didn't see anything good ahead so I began a searching turn to the left. Then I saw it, a beautiful, recently harvested bean field, close along side a farm. I set up my pattern and made one of the best landings I have ever made. I opened the canopy, undid my seat belts, got out, removed my chute and walked the short distance to the farm buildings.

I was cautious. I knew every farm has a dog and most of them don't take kindly to unexpected visitors. Sure enough he came out from around the corner of a building barking and snarling. As a runner I read dog pretty good. This one for all his nastiness was carrying his tail between his legs. I ignored him. The screen door of the farmhouse opened and out stepped a really big farmer. He was a giant of a man with a big black beard. The dog went into friendly mode and disappeared.

"I hope you are a friendly farmer," I said with a big forced smile on my face. "What's the problem?" he asked. "I just made a forced landing in your harvested bean field" I told him. "Come on in." I breathed a sigh of relief.

There were about half a dozen farmers sitting around the kitchen table drinking coffee, probably laying out the day's work. They were a little surprised to see me. "Mary, get this fella a cup of coffee and hand him the phone," the farmer said.

We discussed the situation for a while and a plan was made. Mary had to take the pickup into the next town which was called "Paw Paw," to pick up some tractor parts and said I could go along and she would drop me off at "Caseys," a general store, gas station sort of place, where my wife could meet me.

I called my wife and told her what had happened. Dort doesn't drive so she called a neighbor to see if they would haul her out there. She called back in about fifteen minutes and it was all set up.

Everybody piled out of the house and went out to the ship; even the dog came along. I didn't need eight people and a dog to help me move that little airplane but they were all excited about it. I finally convinced them that if one of them would grab a wing tip and hold the wings level I could grab the prop and pull the plane into the farmyard. Then there ensued a rather heated discussion as to who was the most qualified to hold the wings level and for awhile I thought there might be a fist fight. I don't recall how it was finally settled but it was.

The procession moved slowly towards the farmyard and all the while I fielded questions. "How fast this little bugger go?" "How big is the motor?" "Ain't that propeller too teeny?" They were all very curious and the questions never stopped.

It was getting late and I had to be at work as a flight instructor at Hinckley Soaring at ten that morning. I told the farmer I didn't think I could pick the ship up till tomorrow morning and asked if there if there was some place we could put it where it would be out of the wind?

We got the ship around the barn and into the side yard. The tail was shoved into a corncrib up to the trailing edge of the wings and we tied the wings to the outside walls.

I expressed some concern about the trailing edges being scuffed up on the rough boards. No problem, Mary ran into the house and returned with what looked to me like two brand new blankets. We wrapped the wings in the blankets and secured them to the boards again. Satisfied that my bird was safe for the night I thanked them all for their help. They all stood around beaming and nodding at a job well done.

Mary and I jumped into the truck and headed for Paw Paw. The route there involved lots of turns. I tried to memorize every road sign and landmark along the way. I was wishing I had a pencil and some paper. We got to the Caseys and I jumped out and thanked Mary and she went on her way.

It wasn't long before Dort, the neighbor lady and her husband showed up. The neighbors seemed to be enjoying the whole thing and viewed it as sort of an adventure. After all, how often does one get called upon to rescue a downed pilot? They took me to the glider field and my day began. As luck would have it, it was a long day and any thought of retrieving my ship was out of the question.

The next day Dort and I headed out early with the trailer in tow. We got to Paw Paw all right but finding the farm proved to be a bit of a problem. After driving around for an hour or so I decided to drive back to town to ask for directions. We stopped at a filling station and I asked the only person there if he knew how to get to the Johnson farm? "Sure do," he said, "I was the best man at their wedding." He said he couldn't tell us exactly how to get there but he could draw us a map. He then proceeded to fill an entire page with squiggles and lines but not one word, number or symbol.

I would ask him what the road names were at an intersection and he would just say, "Aw, I don't know but it is about a quarter of a mile past a red barn. Go on down the road a piece till you cross a crick and turn left at the farm with the three blue silos."

When he was done I held the paper up and looked at it. I got the feeling I would never see my "Moni" again. Then I asked him to run through it one more time and I filled in as many details as I could. After thanking him I got back in the car and started out. By golly I found the place!

We pulled into the yard and got out. There didn't seem to be anybody around, not even the dog. I heard a racket down by the silos and I could see someone loading a truck from the silo. We untied the ships' wings from the corncrib and pulled it out. We lined up the trailer, backed out the fuselage dolly, pulled the wings off and slid then into the trailer. Then we used the winch to pull the fuselage on the dolly up into the trailer. In about forty-five minutes we were ready to roll.

While we were doing all this, Joe came by to say that he was sorry that he could not help but he had to get that truck loaded. I told him that Dort and I had done this many times and a third helper wasn't necessary.

I also noticed during this time that Mary got home. We folded the blankets and took them up to the house. I thanked Mary again and tried to give her a ten-dollar bill. "Oh that won't be necessary," she said, "We haven't had this much excitement around here in years." Apparently the phone lines had been humming. She told me that farmers for miles around had been dropping in all afternoon and evening to see the airplane in the corncrib. I could just imagine the conversation, "Yep, this fella in a little airplane just plopped down in Joe's bean field, got it tied up in the corn crib right now." We talked awhile longer and then said goodbye. I stuck the ten under the potted plant on the table.

As we pulled out of the drive we saw Joe walking towards the house. He yelled, "Good bye, drop in anytime."

OUTLANDINGS

When a glider pilot starts out from one airport with the intention of flying several hundred miles and returning to the same airport, they don't always make it. No matter how high the performance of the sailplane or how hot the pilot, it is still a chancy deal. Every sailplane pilot must be prepared to make an out landing.

Sailplanes are designed with the possibility of an outlanding in mind. They are easily disassembled and put into trailers for transporting. The seating is more supine than that of a power plane and they all have four or five point safety harnesses, both of which are easier on the pilot in the event of a hard landing.

Out landings can happen on a variety of terrain. Sometimes they occur on other airports, farm fields, golf courses or any place else the pilot thinks he can land the ship without damaging the glider or injuring himself. Sometimes the pilot doesn't have a lot of choice.

The type of retrieval depends of course on where the pilot lands. If the pilot lands on an airport it is a simple matter for them to call the home field and have a tow plane come out and tow them back home. If the landing is made in a farm field there is still a possibility for them to be towed out, if not then a trailer will be sent out, the ship dissembled, put into the trailer and hauled out.

The Midwest, at least Illinois, offers an abundance of good outlanding sites. Some other parts of the country are not so fortunate. Mountains and forests are not good places to land out.

Fields for out-landings do have an order of preference. First choice after airports would be a field that has been harvested. If the pilot must land in crops, low crops are better than tall. In other words beans are better than corn, especially if the corn has ears on it. A glider hitting an ear of corn at about forty miles an hour won't do itself any good.

Pastures are to be avoided. If the land isn't being planted there must be a reason. Pastures usually contain rocks, stumps, ditches, etc, etc. Pastures with cattle in them are bad news. Even if you land and miss all the cows, you could still be in trouble. Cows are inquisitive creatures and they may damage your glider inadvertently. Pigs are probably even worse. I had a friend who lost control of his radio-controlled glider and it came down in a pigpen. By the time he got to it there was nothing left, the pigs ate it.

Once the pilot has made a successful landing on a farm field he will have a new situation to deal with, the farmer. I really believe most farmers are like the one I encountered in the "Drop In Anytime" of this book. I have heard some stories to the contrary, where the pilot was met by a farmer with a gun or farmers refusing to let a pilot retrieve his ship. Situations sometimes develop that result in litigation.

There are things the pilot can do to ease the situation. Being polite and courteous and a little bit humble goes a long way. If the off field landing occurs close to the home field, an offer of a free glider ride could be made. If crops are damaged, offer to pay for them. One pilot told me of photographing each of the farmers kids sitting in the glider and ended up having supper with the farmers family while waiting for his retrieval crew to show up.

At one time I could account for thirteen outlandings, then I stopped counting. Of the thirteen only three resulted in dealing with a farmer and only one resulted in some crop damage. I heard by the grapevine that the farmer was looking for me. Up to that point I didn't even know who owned the land and frankly felt the damage was so slight that it was not worth finding out. I tried my darndest to contact him by phone. When I finally did reach him and explained the situation, he laughed the whole thing off. I think the fact that I did try hard to contact him and I did apologize and offer to pay for the damage was enough for him.

Farmers are like anybody else. If they feel that they have been wronged in any way they are not happy. If you show that you are trying to do the right thing, everything is cool.

BEAUTY IS IN THE EYE OF THE BEHOLDER

The Midwest landscape in Illinois has no spectacular views, no jutting, jagged, snow capped peaks, no ocean crashing on coral blue reefs or white sandy beeches. Still it has a beauty all its own.

The multi-shaded plots of green crops march in geometric procession, across a tabletop flat land, from horizon to horizon.

Patches of dark woods and small white towns dot the view. It is forever changing with the season, green summer, russet fall, winter white and spring black. Day by day, week by week, month by month, it changes.

Arrow straight rows of crops and arrow straight roads and highways seem to go on forever. Everything is North, South, East, and West. You can measure distance by counting section lines. Each section is a mile. About the only things that run at an angle are rivers, streams; and railroad tracks.

I don't know why I can spend countless hours doing nothing but flying around looking down at it. Maybe I think it is beautiful.

I was going through the commercial exhibits at a local fly-in when someone tapped me on the shoulder and I turned around. It was Joe, my flying friend from the old neighborhood in River Forest, Illinois. We chatted awhile and he asked me if I had a chance to look at that "Piper Colt" and pointed to it on the flight line. Even from where we stood, 100 or more yards away, I could tell I was looking at a beauty queen. Her finish gleamed in the sun.

Joe then went on to describe how it must have had at least forty coats of hand rubbed paint, how there was no ridge to be felt where one color butted up against the other.

Then he told me that every screw was driven in so that all the heads lined up perfectly and on and on. "You know, the guy even has little silk roses woven into the tie-down ropes," he said. I told my friend I would certainly take a look at it. We talked a little longer and then parted.

I started down the line towards the beauty queen and then another plane caught my eye, it was a "Pazmany PL 2." She wasn't a new ship and her bare aluminum skin was dull from being outside many long hours in the elements. The nosebowl, wingtips and the tips of her tail had received a coat of fluorescent orange at one time or another but buy now this had faded out in places to an almost school bus yellow.

I stopped dead in my tracks. Then I began to circle the ship, stopping now and then to enjoy a particular angle. There was something about this plane that really appealed to me. Finally I walked up close and peered inside. The interior was all dull green zinc chromate. In some places of high wear the paint was worn through to reveal shinny aluminum metal. The seat was faded and slightly frayed from hard use. "Perfect," I thought.

After awhile I was able to tear myself away and I turned to look for the beauty queen. I caught a glimpse of her taxing out to the runway. I missed getting to see her. Darn!

I guess it is true what they say, "Beauty is in the eye of the beholder."

THE PITH BALL VARIOMETER

Back in 1977 when I started to build the Mitchell B-10, one of my goals was to be able to climb up to a certain altitude with the engine and then turn it off and soar like an Eagle. I was already a glider pilot and I had never seen a glider that didn't have a variometer, which is a device that tells the pilot if the glider is making the slightest gain or loss of altitude. It is like a super sensitive rate of climb indicator.

The only things that can soar without a variometer are certain types of birds and I am sure they have some sort of a built in variometer. Some people believe a soaring bird can detect "lift" (a rising mass of air) or "sink" (a descending mass of air) with their feathers. Others claim they do it with some sort of hollow device in their skulls, which expands or contracts in relationship to the altitude gain or loss. Still others have other theories but you get the picture.

A good commercial vario would set me back about $350.00; that was a lot of money to me in 77; then I wasn't so well heeled. Now I am better off. I actually own two varios and drink beer in micro breweries where it costs $3.50 a glass and tastes like raspberries.

One day I was talking to a buddy about the high cost of varios when he asked, "Why don't you build one"? He said he was sure he had seen an article in an ancient issue of a soaring magazine on how to build a "Pith Ball Variometer," and he felt sure he could find it. He did and so I did.

The pith ball variometer, which I built, consisted of a rectangular block of plastic about 3 inches long, 1 ½ inches wide and ¾ inches thick. It has two slightly tapering holes going the long way through and in these holes float little balls of Elderberry pith, one colored green (UP) and one colored red (DOWN). To the top or large end of the down tube containing the red ball you attach a small hose leading to a thermos bottle. To the bottom end or small end of the up tube containing the green ball you attach a hose leading to another thermos bottle.

If the aircraft rises the air rushes out of the bottles and blows the red ball down and the green ball up. If the aircraft descends the air rushes into the bottles sucking the red ball up and the green ball down. How ingenious! The rate of rise or descent causes the balls to float higher or lower in the tapered tube. I decided to build it.

Working as a product designer for what was then the nation's largest retailer in the worlds tallest building, (notice I am not using any names here) I had access to many things. I have this reoccurring nightmare that they found out all the things I accessed and they come and take back all that money they gave me when I retired.

One of the things I had access to was the product model shop where there worked this really fine model maker who just happened to be a Nazi. This guy had a solution to all the world's problems, unfortunately they all involved some form of genocide. "Ve should take zem all out in za boat, shoot zem and dump zair bodies in za lake," he would say. If everybody he didn't like were shot and dumped into the lake, you could walk from Chicago to Michigan City Indiana in a straight line and never get your feet wet. I will never ever forget the very first day I was introduced to him. He squinted his eyes and said,"You are French yes?" I told him I was "Vichy French" and that fixed everything.

This guy turned two pins out of brass with the correct taper and we sent them out to have them chrome plated. I built a mold, inserted the pins and cast the rectangular block with casting plastic. When it set up I removed the pins and ended up with two holes of the correct taper, in a block of plastic of the proper dimensions.

Now all I had to do was make the pith balls. One Saturday morning when I was out for a six mile run I happened to run by a forest preserve and guess what I saw? There were the most beautiful elderberry bushes I ever laid eyes on. Later that day I returned with a machete and gathered a good supply of branches. It did occur to me that I might get in a whole lot of trouble standing right next to the road cutting down forest preserve bushes. What would happen if one of the local police saw me, stopped and asked, "Pardon me sir, but what are you doing?" If I were to reply, "Whacking the pith out of these bushes," would he think I was a smart-ass?

I took the branches home and carefully removed the bark and ended up with long ¼ inch diameter rods of spongy pith. These were laid on top of the furnace to dry out for a couple of weeks.

I laid out a 6-inch diameter circle on a piece of 2-inch thick wood and cut it out with a band saw and discarded the plug. The inside of the circle was lined with sandpaper except for the crack where the band saw blade entered the circle. A plywood base was glued to one side and a rubber gasket was fitted to the edges of the other side.

The dry rods of pith were cut into quarter inch cubes and about eight pieces were placed inside the circle. A piece of clear plastic was clamped to the gasket and high-pressure air was blown into the crack. The little pith pieces would dance around like crazy and like magic turn into little pith balls. The longer the air was left on the smaller the balls became. If you held the air on too long you ended up with pith dust. As far as I can figure this stuff isn't good for anything except to inflict a severe bout of sneezing.

At a product engineering show I discovered a company that made light aluminum flasks. They were about the size of thermos bottles and a lot lighter. "Just the thing," I thought. I handed the man at the booth my business card and told him I was working on a very hush hush project and then I told him if this project was a success, we would need thousands of these flasks. I then inquired if it might be possible to get some samples? Boy! Did I get samples.

As it turned out the flasks were useless. I had the assembled gizmo sitting on the desk in my office and had lots of fun with it. If a female employee walked by and spotted the thing and wanted to know what it was, I would tell her it was a device to measure how passionate a woman was. I would tell the lady to gently grasp the flask with both hands and watch the little green ball. I would explain that the higher the ball floated the more passionate they were. The heat from their hands would cause the air in the flask to expand and that would cause the ball to rise off its seat and float up in the tube. They all left the office smiling, confident in the knowledge that they were indeed passionate women. I now realized why I had to use thermos bottles.

Finally the device was completed and I wanted to test it but this was January and the glider field would not be open until April. I couldn't wait; I wanted to test it now. The building I worked in had an express elevator that ran with no stops between the first and the 27th floor. It was a simple matter to compute the distance between floors and using a stopwatch I could determine the feet per minute of vertical travel.

With the thermos bottles in a brown paper bag and tubes and the vario sticking out the top, I began my tests. Entering the elevator in a three-piece business suit and carrying this gadget had a strange effect on the other passengers. They tended to bunch up in the opposite corner and their eyes got large. I wondered if they thought I might demand that the elevator be diverted to Cuba.

Only once in all my ups and downs did anyone speak. The doors just closed and a man asked what that thing was? I replied, "It's a variometer." Silence! He was the last to leave the elevator and just before the doors closed he spun around on his heels and said,"Variometer indeed!"

Finally spring arrived and I was doing lots of flying as a demo pilot at Hinckley Soaring. I would temporarily install the thing in the back seat of a glider when I took someone for a ride. This way I was able to calibrate it and mark the face in the proper increments for lift or sink.

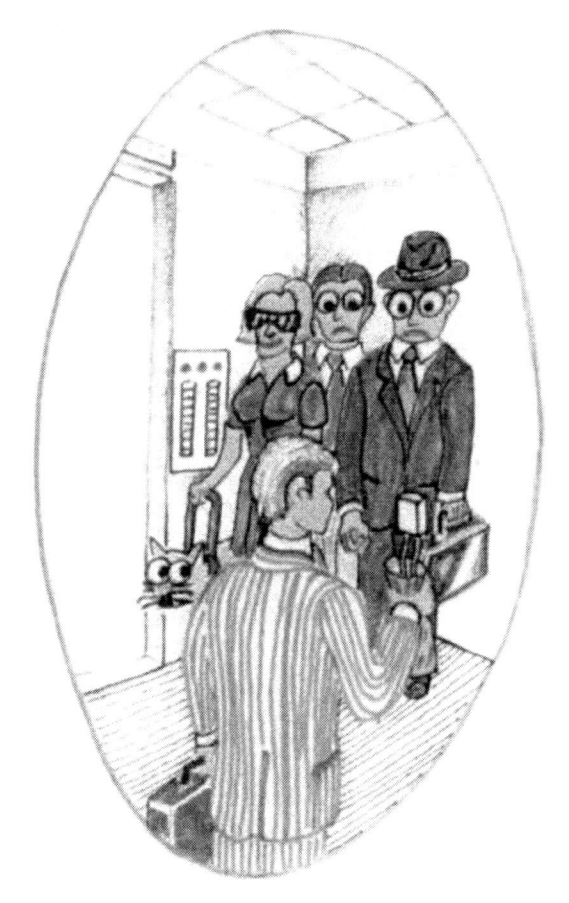

When the Mitchell B-10 was completed I installed it in the wing center section and used it for awhile. It worked very well but like all pith ball variometers it was a little slow. Later on I did buy an electric vario and it was a lot faster. Still I would occasionally glance up to check the old pith ball to make sure the electric wasn't lying.

There is a story and I don't know if it is true but it is a good story anyway. Back in the early days of soaring when flights were measured in minutes not hours, a soaring contest was held. A German pilot was observed climbing into his glider with a large paper bag. All the other pilots laughed at him and thought he was taking his lunch. They also thought he was quite egotistic to think he would be up long enough to need sustenance. In that bag was his secret weapon, a pith ball vario. Well, he won the contest hands down. I don't know how long he was up but they claim he dropped a few beer bottles out of the glider. Maybe he did have his lunch in that bag too.

BUILDING YOUR OWN

As a young boy building model airplanes I would dream of the day when I would build a real airplane. Every now and then I would bang some boards together in the form of an airplane, some of these would have working controls. I would move the stick and the rudder bar and strings would make other small boards move about like control surfaces. I would sit on these things and make motor noises for hours. In 1977 I began to make the dream of building a real airplane come true. Today I am presently working on my third real airplane and yes, I still sit in the uncompleted thing and make motor noises.

To me, building and flying your own aircraft has got to be one of life's greatest experiences. It is an experience that very few people ever achieve. The "EAA," (Experimental Aircraft Association), an organization devoted to home-building aircraft, has at this time 170,000 members. There are currently about 2200 registered home built aircraft on the FAA records. This apparently means that less than 2% of the members have ever built an airplane. And if you take into consideration that most people who build one aircraft go on to build another, the percentage is even less. Of course not everyone in the EAA wants to build an airplane. Maybe you have to be a little bit crazy!

In the course of building an airplane certain problems arise, like, where am I going to store these two fourteen foot wings I just completed? How and where will I paint this thing? How will I make this part without the proper tools? At times like these my wife will say, "Ron, why didn't you think this thing through before you began?" I really believe if a person sat down and contemplated all the problems that would arise in the course of building an airplane, they would never start. If one were to think about all the blood, sweat and tears, all the time and money, it would seem an insurmountable task. Sometimes you just have to jump right in.

People have many reasons not to build an airplane. They don't have the skill. You can learn if you want to. They don't have the space. People have built planes in living rooms, carports, basements, and I even heard of one guy who rented a semi trailer and built it in there. They don't have the tools. Tools can be borrowed, rented, picked up at garage sales, or purchased one at a time. Hand tools will do the job of some power tools; it just takes a little longer. They don't have the time. How much time do you watch TV everyday? They don't have the money. You can purchase a set of plans and buy a small piece of aluminum or a few sticks of wood and get started. You don't have to pay for the whole thing at once. How good are you at scrounging? They have a wife who doesn't want them to build an airplane. Oh Oh! You got a real problem. I can think of a couple of solutions but all of them are drastic and one of them is illegal. There is a joke that goes around among home-builders, the wife says to her husband, "Either that plane goes or I go," the husband replies, "Hell, that's an easy choice."

Incidentally, not all homebuilders are men. I once read of a woman who built a plane in her living room. Apparently she had an understanding husband. A cooperative mate is the one thing you really need to build a plane, whether male or female.

The way you build an airplane is to build one small piece at a time. Maybe it is just a bell-crank or a gusset. It is just a small piece of metal with a few holes drilled in it. After a while you have boxes of these small parts sitting around and so you put a few of them together and you end up with a sub assembly. Then you stick a few of these together and you end up with a rudder or an aileron or some other part that actually looks like a part of an airplane. You put these parts together and one day you walk out into the garage and there sits something that definitely looks like an airplane. You walk around it and no matter what angle you view it from it is not a knickknack shelf or a birdhouse. Then you say, "Oh my God, what have I created!"

It is at this point that a decision has to be made. You have been so intent on the trees that you didn't notice the forest growing up around you. You have built an airplane and airplanes are for flying. Are you going to fly that thing? If you spend a lot of time looking at the personal for sale adds in the back of home-building magazines, you will sometimes see an ad that goes like this: Project for sale, "Super Duper XX, 95% completed, all materials to complete, $19,000.00, illness forces sale." Call XXX XXX XXXX. I often wonder if that illness is a pair of really cold feet?

Are you really ready to become a test pilot? That is what you are about to become if you persevere. There is an out though; perhaps you can talk someone else into testing it for you. In a way it is not a bad idea, you are emotionally involved with this thing and he is not. If something should go wrong up there he is not going to waste any time trying to save the ship, he is going to get out of there. I just couldn't ever bring myself to go this route. To me this seems comparable to getting someone else to take your new bride on your honeymoon.

After all those years of working and dreaming the big day arrives. You find yourself sitting at the end of this long, lonely runway, it is just you, the ship, the sky, and God. You think about all those glue joints, all those rivets, all those bolts and nuts. You slowly roll the power on and go for it. There is nothing in this world like it.

SHOPPING

Occasionally while building an airplane I will be faced with a problem that I know can be solved if I had a certain widget or a thingama-bob. I just know this thing exists out there somewhere, I just don't know what it is or what it is used for. So I spend all kinds of time pushing a shopping cart up and down the isles of some store looking for this thing. I usually look for it in a hardware store although you would be surprised what you can find in a place like "Mary Jane's Fabrics" or "Ben Franklin's Crafts."

Sometimes the help in these stores becomes uneasy when I am on one of these expeditions. They see me slowly cruising the isles, fondling the merchandise and it makes them nervous. Some clerk will ask, "May I help you sir?" "No, I don't think so." "Well, what are you looking for?" "I don't really know." This just drives them nuts. In one store in particular I am sure they thought I was a shoplifter. I kept catching them peeking down the isles at me. Now when I visit my local small town hardware I just tell them I will be looking around in the aircraft department and they pretty much ignore me. I overheard one of the clerks tell a customer that I was crazy, I was building an airplane.

One of the greatest joys of my life is to find some object, which perfectly fits a need for which it is totally unrelated. When I got my "Moni" motor-glider completed to the point where I could sit in it and make motor noises, I discovered a problem. The sitting position in that aircraft is quite supine, you are practically lying down in the thing. This is actually a very pleasant way to fly except for the fact that you have to hold your head erect to be able to see over the nose of the ship. This is a very tiring thing to do and it doesn't take long before it becomes a real pain in the neck, really. I needed something to rest my head on.

I thought about building a headrest by cutting a circular piece of foam rubber and sewing some sort of a cover over it but I just knew there was something out there that I could buy to do the job.

One day while I was shopping at "Farm and Fleet," a rather unique store where you can buy a tool to castrate your bull while your wife is buying a new blouse, I wandered into the plumbing section. I noticed a row of toilet plungers on a shelf. They were round and made of soft rubber and so I began to try them on my head. I also noticed a young lady who was stocking the shelves was watching me with a very strange look on her face. I finally found one that was just right and put it in my shopping cart.

Now all I needed was a cover for it. In the automobile section I discovered a lambs wool buffing bonnet which is used to buff out paint. It was the right size and it had a drawstring to secure it in place. I put it on the toilet plunger and tried it on my head for size and comfort. Perfect! That same gal came around the corner and caught me in the act and got that same strange look on her face again.

Whenever someone looks at my "Moni" I always point out the headrest because I am so proud of it. Some of my friends have told me it is only fitting that I should use a toilet plunger as a headrest considering the contents of my head. It's so nice to have friends.

One of my friends has considerable experience with the same type of engine that I am using in the "Moni." He told me that he had better results using a different spark plug than the ones that came with the engine. I decided to take his advice, there was one slight problem. The plugs supplied with the engine were what they call "shorty" plugs and the ones I wanted to use had a longer porcelain insulator on them.

In order to get the cowl to fit I had to drill holes in it to clear the porcelain insulators. This was not only an unsightly solution but also an aerodynamic abomination. I had to find some sort of streamlined plug covers.

Once again I knew there was something out there that would be just the right thing, so back to "Farm and Fleet." I wandered the aisles in vain until I got to the auto section. Bingo! There I saw some truck cab clearance lights that looked like they were made to do the job. They were very streamlined, like one half of a teardrop. Not only were these things aerodynamic, they had these lenses that could be removed with one screw and that allowed me to be able to check the plugs without removing the entire cowl as all the other guys did.

These things catch everyone's eye and they all want to know what they are for. I tell them I am helping the FAA experiment with turn signals for aircraft and so far it looks good and they will probably be required on all aircraft next year. None of the pilots believe me but quite a few civilians do. Maybe it's not such a bad idea. Maybe I should take out a patent.

IT WAS GOOD ENOUGH FOR THE LUFTWAFFE

After WWI the treaty of Versailles prohibited Germany from building or flying powered aircraft. It said nothing about gliders. It is said that most of the Luftwaffe pilots got their flight training in gliders first, before they learned to fly power when the war started. Maybe that wasn't such a bad idea? Maybe all of us should have to do it that way.

Although I got my license in gliders first, I did have a student ticket in power before that. Glider training is more stick and rudder oriented than power training. There are a lot less gauges to worry about and you don't have that big, noisy, stinky thing, hanging out in front to distract you. You have to pay a lot more attention to your surroundings, instead of staring at a lot of needles on dials.

On the nine o'clock news I watch a reporter interviewing a farmer who was an eyewitness to a lightplane crash. He is standing there in a plaid shirt and bib overalls with a ball cap advertising some brand of tractor. "Yep," he says, "I heard the engine quit and she just came right down and crashed."

The reporter looks into the camera and says, "The pilot and passenger were both killed in the crash." There is a shot of the crumpled plane lying in a bean field that is perfectly flat and about a mile square and I wonder why the airplane crashed. There are some places where if the engine quits you will probably hurt yourself bad, like over a forest, mountains, or city, but a bean field?

A Cessna 150 at 65 MPH with zero flaps and wind speed and the propeller windmilling has about an eight to one glide ratio. If you stop the prop, it will be better than that. If you glide into a bean field at that angle you may bend the plane a little and maybe you will get a few bumps and bruises but you should be able to walk away from the landing.

Maybe it is just the way power flying is taught these days by some instructors? My old power instructor, "Dutch," taught me to fly the landing pattern so that if the engine did quit I would still be able to glide into the airport. He taught me lots of other things that I don't believe are being taught today.

Most of all the power training I received the second time around was off the sod runway at Hinckley airport, which was without a control tower. One day as a student pilot I decided to shoot some landings at a tower controlled airport.

I called the tower and entered the pattern just fine. When I got to the point where I thought I should turn onto the base leg I turned. It was then that the gal in the tower began to scream, "Cessna niner niner seven, fly east, fly east." I did and then I saw why she was so excited. There way out in front of me were other aircraft flying on their downwind and base legs! They were so far away I could barely see them. I wondered if they would reach the airport if their engines quit? In fact, I wondered if they would land in the same county that the airport was in if their engines quit? It wasn't that crowded and I couldn't understand why they were doing that.

I drive past that airport many times and see a lone aircraft in the pattern turn final so far out that there is no way they will make the field if they have an engine out. They would have to be about 600 feet up if there is any wind at all and around here there usually is.

One day Dutch told me to maintain a normal climb till I hit two thousand feet and then close the throttle completely and make a 45 degree banked, 180 degree turn, at 65 MPH. I did as I was told and then he asked me how much altitude we lost? It was 350 feet. A real good thing to know if your engine quits on climb out and you wonder about turning back to the runway.

Another little trick he used to pull, was to take two big suction cups out of his pocket and attach them to the faces of the altimeter and the airspeed indicator so both were completely covered and could not be used. Then he would tell me to enter the landing pattern and land the plane. You would have nothing to go by, except how things looked, how the ship sounded, how it felt.

Dutch was not only a power instructor; he was a glider pilot too. He knew that when the engine quits in a power plane you are simply flying a glider, not a very good glider but a glider never the less. There really isn't any reason to kill yourself.

RUDDER FLUTTER

A friend of mine who got me into glider flying in the first place was a man about twelve years older than me. One day he confided in me that he was susceptible to leg cramps or what is commonly known as "Charlie Horse." He told me that his biggest fear was that one day when he was flying he would experience control surface flutter in the rudder and then at the same instant get a "Charlie Horse." He felt he would not be able to stop the flutter because he would not be able to apply any pressure to the rudder petals.

I didn't know a whole lot about control surface flutter at the time and although I thought his chances were rather remote that he would experience both rudder flutter and a leg cramp at the same time, I did think it was possible.

Shortly after I began to fly radio control gliders, I got a glider so high up in a thermal one day that I feared I would lose it. I tried to get the ship down by putting it into a spiral dive, the worse possible thing I could have done. The glider went past it's redline speed, I heard a buzzing sound and the ship broke up. I knew I had experienced flutter when I found the control surfaces some distance from the main wreckage.

My friend did get to solo and got his student glider pilots' license but then quit flying. Just how much his fear of Charlie Horses and rudder flutter had to do with his decision to quit I'll never know.

Years went by and I became a flight instructor. I learned a whole lot more about control surface flutter by reading about it and I hoped that would be the only way I would ever learn about it.

Occasionally I would get a student that was rather unique in one way or another. This one was unique in two ways, he was paying for his lessons by collecting discarded aluminum cans along the highway and he was strung tighter than a banjo.

He was a tall lanky kid and I liked him. He informed me that he was building a glider and when I asked him what it was to be constructed of, he told me it was all aluminum. Somehow I got this strange vision of all these aluminum cans riveted together and flying around.

I never met anyone who was as nervous as he was. He would latch onto the controls with a death grip and since he was bigger and stronger than I was I had a heck of a time with him. I began to wonder if I shouldn't start carrying a large heavy object to render him unconscious, in case he really locked up on me. I tried everything to get him to relax. I would demonstrate to him that the glider was quite capable of flying along all by itself, for a rather extended period of time, if you just simply let it alone.

To prove that this was true, I would tell him to take his hands and feet off the controls and I would watch to see that he did. Then I would put my hands on his shoulders to prove that I no longer had my hands on the stick and I would swear to him that my feet were not on the rudder petals, and they weren't. The old glider would drift along for a few minutes, then start to meander off into a gentle turn to the left or right. After awhile I would ask him to take control again. This demonstration would have the desired effect of getting him to loosen up on the controls. It would last for about three minutes and then I could feel the stiffness start to return to the stick and rudder pedals. Lesson after lesson went by and I just couldn't get him to relax no matter what I did.

He was flying the glider one-day and shortly after we got off tow I felt a strange buzz in the rudder pedals. I couldn't imagine what it was and for a moment I thought the dreaded rudder flutter was about to get me. I asked him to take his feet off the pedals and sure enough the buzz went away. When he put his feet back on the rudder petals the buzz returned. I don't know what the frequency of that buzz was, but it had to be about sixty cycles a second. Whatever it was I didn't think it was humanly possible to tap your foot that fast.

I don't know whatever happened to him. Like a lot of people he drifted in and out of my life and left a small impression. It was too bad that he quit because he wasn't that bad a pilot. I don't know if his nervousness finally got to him or maybe the bottom dropped out of the aluminum can market?

THE MANAGER

Over the years that I have worked as a flight instructor in gliders at Hinckley Soaring, I worked for many different managers. Most of the time they were young men considerably less than half my age. Most of them were still in college or had just graduated. In a way they were my bosses and I got along well with all of them. I like working with young people and I feel it keeps me young. If you want to get old fast, work with a bunch of older men.

It seems all of them had the same dream, to become airline pilots. They were all building time. Breaking into the airlines is not a very easy thing to do but most of these guys made it one way or another. They would stick around for a few years and then move on to some other flying job. Some of them became corporate pilots, bush pilots, military pilots but they all got a job doing what they loved, flying.

I have heard stories of young men getting jobs with fly by night outfits flying canceled checks or small parts. They fly in weather when the birds are walking. They fly in ships that are over gross, out of CG and with a squawk list as long as your arm. If they refuse to take the flight there is another young man that will and they will go to the bottom of the list. They are all building time, chasing the dream.

Many times when some kid's father finds out I am a flight instructor they will tell me that their son wants to be an airline pilot because he loves airplanes. They ask me what I think about that and if I have any advice. I tell them to try and talk the kid into becoming a dermatologist or a dentist. That way they can make lots of money, buy their own airplane and fly all they want to. I know if the kid really has the dream, my advice falls on deaf ears.

There is a lot of responsibility to the job of manager at the glider field. The manager sometimes has to make a decision that is not popular with the customer. The customer may have gray hair, have a lot more money and think he has a lot more smarts. It is a good experience for the young man. Sometimes I am consulted on some of these decisions. The manager probably consults me because I have gray hair, a lot more money, and he thinks I have a lot more smarts. We usually work something out.

One day when the wind was directly across the runway and blowing 15, gusting to 25 a customer showed up to fly the Grob-103 which has a maximum crosswind component of 12 MPH.

The manager told him he couldn't fly because of the wind and he became quite irate. He said he had driven a long way to get here, he had the ship scheduled, he had flown the ship in stronger winds than these and on and on. The manager asked me what I thought and I said I didn't know. I told the customer I would call the owner of the operation and ask him what to do. I knew what he would say but I didn't know how cleverly he would say it.

The owner told me to tell the customer to go to the bank and have a certified check made out to Hinckley Soaring for $32,000.00, give the check to the manager and he could fly the ship all he wanted to. The customer didn't want to do that.

There were a lot of days when we couldn't fly because the weather was too bad. The manager and I would sit around and do a lot of hanger flying. Sometimes we would discuss aerodynamics or teaching methods or other things aeronautical. I learned a lot from these kids. Sometimes we would discuss girls. I learned a lot from these kids.

Most of the managers I worked with were smart, ambitious, conscientious and hard working. They didn't get paid a lot of money for what they were doing and the responsibility they bore.

They were enjoying what they were doing. They were chasing a dream.

NAMING YOUR SHIP

It seems everyone names their boat and I have seen some pretty crazy things on the back of transoms. It isn't really necessary to name your airplane but some people do.

The first airplane I built was an ultralight, the "Mitchell B-10." It was a flying wing and didn't have a tail. For the first year I flew it, it didn't have a name. People would give me pictures of it flying overhead. It was yellow and the sun would shine through its wings. It looked like a big butterfly. The ship was made of spruce, covered with cloth and only weighed two hundred and eleven pounds. I decided if Howard Hughes could have a "Spruce Goose," I could have a "Spruce Butterfly." I painted a Monarch butterfly in the center of the wing's leading edge.

The second ship I built was the "Moni" motorglider. It was painted in a color scheme of a military trainer and I decided to add a little nose art to the cowl. I did some research but couldn't come up with just the right thing.

I am an avid skier and I hope I never have to make a choice between skiing or flying, it just might be skiing. After a hard day on the slopes I get thirsty. I try to avoid the ski area watering holes which are usually done up in a vacuum formed "Bavarian" motif. I like to drink in real bars. While driving home from the slopes I saw this low, ugly, cinder-block building with a sign on the roof that said "TOMS." The place seemed to have one door and one window and the window had a neon sign that said "BEER." I wheeled into the muddy parking lot. As I walked through the door the reek of stale beer and cigar smoke greeted my nose, I had found a home.

After my eyes became accustomed to the gloom, I crawled up on a barstool and ordered a shot of peppermint Schnapps and a draft beer chaser. The gal who served it had seen better days. She had a whiskey voice and as I found out later, a real bad case of "Potty Mouth."

The back-bar was covered with all kinds of signs and I began to read them. One of them caught my eye. It was in the form of a European road sign, a round white disk with a red boarder and a red angular slash crossing the black silhouette of a bull making "Do Do." The message was clear. Perfect, I thought, I had found my nose art! That is how my ship became the "NO BULL SPECIAL."

My third ship, the one I am presently working on must be named "DORT," my wife's nickname, at least that is what it says in 27' letters on the top of one wing and the bottom of the other. I figure that after going through three of these things with me she deserves some recognition.

PARACHUTE

Sometimes things work out in the strangest way. In 1977 I started to build a flying wing ultralight called the "Mitchell B-10" and I finished it and flew it for the first time in 1980. Sometime in about the middle of the project I began to really look at the thing. It was constructed primarily of lots and lots of little sticks glued together. I began to think about all those hundreds and hundreds of little glue joints. I decided, maybe I should have a parachute.

It must have been about 1978 when the Soaring Society Of America held its annual convention in Chicago in a convention center out by O'Hare airport and I decided to attend.

As I walked from display to display I noticed that the Security Parachute Company was having a special show price on their chutes. I think the price was about $400.00 and I believe I had about ten dollars in my pocket at the time and I didn't as yet carry any plastic. That was a real good price and I wanted to buy it. I didn't want to drive all the way home to get the money. What to do?

After awhile I spotted "Al" the chief honcho at Hinckley Soaring and I asked him if he would write me a check for the amount of the chute. Al looked a little surprised but after I explained, he wrote the check and told me to tell the people at the chute display not to cash it for three days.

I returned home that evening with my new parachute, much to my wife's surprise. I modeled it for her. She didn't seem to be very impressed. I put on my helmet and goggles, then I put on my boots and tucked the pants legs into the top of my boots. I stood in front of the mirror, "cool." I thought. I threw the chute on the floor in the closet and forgot about it.

Al purchased a "Schweizer 1-35"and put it on the line for rental at

Hinckley Soaring. I thought it was beautiful and I wanted to fly it. There was only one problem, there was a placard on the instrument panel that said the minimum pilot weight was a little more than I weighed, of course I could carry ballast. Then a little light went on in my head, heck, Why not wear my chute? I had a 16-pound parachute lying on the floor of my closet doing nothing, may as well wear it.

And so I began wearing my chute whenever I flew the SGS 1-35. I was only wearing it for ballast, I never expected to use it. Then on June 20, 1980, at 5000 feet over Hinckley Soaring I had a problem flying the 1-35 that resulted in my bailing out of that ship.

So Al loaned me the money to buy a parachute which I used to bail out of his glider. Sometimes things work out in the strangest way.

BIG-BONED WOMAN

It was a hot muggy mid-west morning and I wasn't exactly looking forward to the day. Glider cockpits are not air-conditioned and the office wasn't either.

At about 10:30 she walked through the door. She was a big-boned gal in a white pair of slacks and a purple halter-top and lots and lots of perfume. We discussed rides and she decided on a two thousand-foot tow in our standard training glider.

As we walked down the line of gliders towards the one we would be using, she informed me that her husband was in the Army and she said she was having all kinds of fun while he was gone.

A guy in an eighteen wheeler rolling down route 30 beside the field must have spotted her as we walked along, he laid on the air horn and she waived gaily in reply. Her attitude was infectious and by the time we got to the ship I was feeling a lot better. I guess you would describe her as "bubbly," the kind of woman it is fun to be around.

I untied the glider and was trying to pull it out of its tie down spot by the nose maneuvering handle. The main wheel was stuck in a hole and I couldn't get it out. I asked her if she would grab the wing strut and help pull. She pulled all right, the glider sprang out of the hole and damn near ran over me!

We got the ship out on the runway and swung it around to face the wind. I got her aboard and as I was strapping her in I briefly mentioned that those rudder pedals up front and that stick between her legs were what controlled the glider. I didn't go into great detail because it was obvious she just wanted to have fun.

After I got her situated, I opened the door to the aft cockpit and began to straighten out the seat belts before getting in.

I wanted to check the stick for freedom of movement and since the front and back stick are interconnected, whatever I did with the back stick happened up front. I moved the stick full right, full left, full forward and then full back. That big-boned gal said, "Woo Ho Ho."

I CALLS UM LIKE I SEES UM

It was a mid-week day and although the weather was beautiful and the soaring good, we had little business. About two in the afternoon they walked into the office and since I was behind the counter I waited on them. He said they wanted to go for a glider ride. I explained the various types of flights we offered and he chose the higher performance ship and a three thousand-foot tow for both flights.

I wrote up the bill, took the money and handed him the change and a receipt. Then I asked, "Do you want to go up first or shall I take your daughter?" Big mistake! He glared at me and with a voice that would freeze water informed me, "She is not my daughter." She just stood there and smiled.

I was flabbergasted. I stood there with my mouth open. Now I wish I had come up with a snappy reply. At least I could have winked and given him a sly smile. I did nothing.

On his flight the atmosphere in the cockpit was rather frosty. I thought, perhaps I would do better with her. She seemed to be rather vacuous and I couldn't tell if she enjoyed it or not. Both flights were bummers as far as I was concerned. I really felt bad.

Perhaps I should install a large sign somewhere I couldn't possibly miss it, saying, "Engage brain before operating mouth," or maybe, "Consider all possibilities."

AIRIAL SURVEILLANCE

It had to be the weirdest phone call I ever got while working at Hinckley Soaring.

I was just unlocking the door to the office one morning to begin another day of work when the phone began to ring. I got the door open and caught the phone on the fifth bounce. The voice of a middle-aged lady was on the other end.

The lady wanted to know if Hinckley airport was an ultralight field. I told her it wasn't but occasionally some ultralights land here. Then she wanted to know if I knew any ultralight pilots who would like to make some money? My ears perked up and it was at this point that I darn near told her that I flew an ultralight. For some reason I didn't mention it.

I assumed she wanted to go for a ride and I asked her if that was what she wanted? "No" she said, "that is not what I want, but I do have a problem. I need an ultralight pilot who is good at flying and also good with a camera and a telephoto lens."

Then she explained her problem. She claimed that the neighbor man was stalking her. She said every time she backed her car out of the garage he would jump into his car and follow her all over town. She said she had reported him to the police but they said they couldn't do anything until she had proof. They told her they couldn't afford to assign an officer full time to her case in the hopes of catching him red-handed.

The lady wanted to set up a sting. She would call the pilot at an appointed time and have him fly over her house.

When he was on station she would jump in her car and start driving. If the stalker followed she would somehow signal the pilot and then head out to some secluded country road where the pilot would do his thing. He would swoop down out of the sky like a falcon on his unsuspecting pray, all the while firing his camera. Hopefully he would get some great shots of both cars in the same frame, the crazed sweaty face of the stalker and also a nice clear shot of the guy's license plate.

I began to think I was the one who was being set up. I thought one of the younger tow pilots was getting his mother to do this to me. The more I listened however the more I became convinced that this woman was for real.

Then I began to get some real fiendish ideas of my own. I did have the phone numbers of some ultralight pilots and also the number of an ultralight field so why not? --- Naw, too dirty. I also began to wonder how they would retaliate.

OH, TO HEAR THE COWS MOO!

Of all the things I have flown, I sometimes feel that I loved my "Mitchell Wing B-10" ultralight the most. It was a 34-foot flying wing with an aluminum tube hang cage slung below. Sixteen-inch bicycle wheels were used as landing gear and a 12 HP go-cart engine propelled the thing. The whole thing weighed about 175 lbs empty and with me aboard the gross weight was around 326 lb. That included my parachute and seven quarts of fuel.

Talk about communing with nature, if I flew low over a farmhouse in the morning, I could smell coffee and bacon.

If I flew through a thin wisp of cloud, I not only saw it, I could feel the moisture on my face and could taste it on my tongue. Visibility was practically unlimited for 360 degrees around and below. The biggest things in my view were my boots. Of course upward visibility wasn't very good with that big wing overhead.

There was one sense I was deprived of however; I couldn't hear a damn thing. This was a self-imposed depravation. With that go-cart engine just a few feet behind my head screaming at eight thousand

RPM, I didn't want to hear anything. I wore a pair of earplugs and a motorcycle helmet and still it was pretty noisy.

It was when I was gliding or soaring with the engine off that I really missed not being able to hear. I would look down on a train snaking along the tracks and wish I could hear the clickity-clack of the wheels on the track and the whistle blow when the engineer laid on it. I wanted to hear the cars on the highway below. I wanted to hear the cows moo in the pasture. I was afraid to take off my helmet and remove the ear plugs while trying to fly the darn thing. I was afraid I might drop something.

Then one day, as I was reading an ultralight flying magazine, I saw an ad for a new helmet. This helmet was like nothing I had ever seen. It had retractable sound deadening ear cups, a sun visor and a full-face shield. I was impressed and although it was rather expensive I decided I couldn't live without it. This helmet would solve my problem of not being to hear when gliding or soaring.

I decided that I would be able to raise the ear cups and by tying the earplugs to a string yoke I could remove them with one simple pull of the string. At last, I would be able to hear the cows moo! I sent my check in and waited impatiently for delivery. It sort of reminded me of the time I sent those cereal box tops and twenty-five cents in for that "Jack Armstrong" secret decoder ring.

When it did arrive I was very anxious to try it out. On the very first flight I discovered some discouraging things about this helmet. Because the face shield was mounted on the detachable sun visor, it was some distance out in front of my face; it acted like a rudder. If I moved my head slightly to one side of dead center, the wind would snap it full over with quite a bit of force and it took some effort to get my head turned back again. I landed and removed the face shield and visor and put my goggles back on.

On the next flight I climbed up to two thousand feet over a pasture full of cows and shut the engine down. I felt sure some of them must have been mooing. I retracted the ear cups and yanked on the string attached to the ear plug and what I heard scared the hell out of me.

That 1.7 ounce Dacron dress liner fabric that I covered the wing with was drumming like crazy. I couldn't believe it remained attached to the wing structure. It sounded like thunder. Every open end of the aluminum tubes of the hang cage and every drilled hole that was unfilled in those tubes was emitting a sound that ranged from a high pitched whistle to a low moan. Each time I changed aircraft attitude they would all change. It was like flying around inside a pipe organ.

I was really disappointed. I replaced my earplugs and lowered the ear cups and I never did that again. Recently I have been using the helmet for skiing and it works fine. I guess it wasn't a total loss.

LOST PROPELLER

With the engine idling on my Mitchell B-10, I glided into the left hand traffic pattern for a landing on runway 09 at Hinckley Soaring. It was a long glide so I decided to clear the engine. Advancing the throttle a little I heard the engine respond but something was missing. I tried again, no thrust! I turned around in my seat as much as possible and looked back and sure enough I could not see the propeller. I had somehow lost my prop! After landing I turned off the runway to one side and shut down. I undid my seat belts, got out and walked around to the back of the ship. Nothing!

A single cylinder engine driving a two bladed propeller through a reduction unit using cog belts, sets up a lot of torsional vibration. In order to tame this vibration I had installed a "Flexadyne Unit" and it did the job quite well. The metal shaft that drove the unit, which drove the prop, had crystallized and broken off. The whole ball of wax had fallen off.

Since I had begun my glide quite high and some distance from the field, I had no idea where my propeller could be.

I decided perhaps it had come off in the landing pattern as that is where I had first discovered it was missing. I talked Al into taking me up in one of the tow planes and we drug the landing pattern several times. At the speed we had to fly to keep from falling out of the sky and looking down on eight foot high corn, it soon became apparent that finding a needle in a hay stack would probably be a lot easier than finding my prop in that corn field. I gave up.

I decided perhaps I should run an ad in the local newspaper but soon thought better of that idea. What if my prop was sticking in the top of some farmer's prize-winning heifer? What if some farmer found it with his $180,000 combine while harvesting his crop? I could just imagine what it would do to his combine. After awhile I decided the best course of action was to just carve a new propeller. I could replace the cog belt drive with a "V" belt drive to take care of the vibration problems and just let it go at that.

At the end of each skydiving season, the guy who owned the jump school would visit each farmer whose crops had sustained damage from an errant parachutist. He would make a peace offering with a bottle of booze or a ham or something.

It was on one such visit, after the farmer and the jump school owner had talked for awhile and probably sampled the booze, that the farmer said, "Say Martha, go out in the shed and bring that propeller I found in here."

The owner of the jump school said he had never seen such a thing before and that he had no idea what type of ship it could have come from or who owned it. The farmer didn't want it so he gave it to him. He took the prop back to the jump school and hung it on the wall, where it remained for the entire winter.

When spring came, one of the glider pilots went into the jump school office to have his chute repacked for the coming soaring season and saw the prop on the wall. He asked the owner why my prop was hanging there? The owner said he didn't even know it was my prop but he bet I would like to have it back. The glider pilot took it back to the soaring school office.

When I arrived at Hinckley Soaring the first time that spring, someone told me that my prop was in the office. I rushed in and sure enough there it was none the worse for wear. Oh, it needed a light sanding and a coat of paint but that was all.

Apparently that heavy flexadyne unit made it spin down like a helicopter. I'll bet it cut a nice 42-inch diameter hole in that corn.
I was happy as a clam! Nobody's cow got killed, nobody's combine got wrecked and I got my propeller back.

FAMILIARITY BREEDS CONTEMPT

Maybe it is possible to fly too much. Maybe too many hours in your logbook is a bad thing.

As an instructor and a demo pilot for Hinckley Soaring I got lots of time in lots of different gliders. In the course of a day I might make as high as fifteen flights in six different ships of three different types.

The Grob 103 had a mouse problem. Mice seemed to love to get in that glider and make pee pee. The owner of that ship had read somewhere that mice will not walk on stainless steel so he installed a 24 inch square concrete pad with a stainless steel plate on top for the main wheel to rest on. The tail wheel was jacked up so mice couldn't get in there.

I hated to have to move that big plastic cow of a glider on the ground. It weighed 794 pounds and I weighed 149. I got into a bad habit. I would land normally and then taxi down the field and make a wide sweeping turn into the parking spot. There was about six feet of room to spare on each side of my glider wing tips.

Many times I would stop with the wheel on that pad and the times I missed, I didn't miss by much. It was then an easy task to get the wheel on the pad and swing the tail 180 degrees around and tie the beast down. I didn't do this to show off because most of the time there was no one there to see me do it. I was just lazy. The more I did this the more I became confident that I could do it.

If I could do it with the Grob, I could do it with a Schweizer 2-33A. It was even easier because the wheel sat in a small depression. All you had to do was aim for the hole, slowly apply the brake and the wheel would fall into the hole.

By now you must know where this story is going. On a crowded weekend day when there must have been about one hundred people on the porch watching me, I aimed the 2-33A for the hole right next to the porch. As I began to apply the brake I made a very interesting discovery, I didn't have any! The ship hit the hole and bounced out again. It continued about 25 feet to the edge of the parking lot, jumped the rail road tie boarder of the lot and hit a car. There are no words to explain how I felt at that moment.

Upon close examination, there was no damage to the car and only slight damage done to the fiberglass nose of the glider. There was a whole lot or damage done to ego. I don't know how I survived the rest of that day.

Now when a lot of people gather on the porch to do some hangar flying, do you think they talk about all the times I parked the Grob with the wheel on that four square foot stainless steel pad? How much would you bet that someone doesn't mention the time I taxied out into the parking lot and hit a car?

There are a lot of things in life I don't do anymore and taxiing a glider into its parking spot is one of them.

TOAST

Not all my flight instructor memories are made of sunshine and laughter, some of them are sad and this is one of those.

I couldn't believe my eyes when I first saw him and his mother walk around the corner of the trailer. I was sitting at the picnic table and even at that distance I knew there was something wrong with this kid, something bad wrong. He looked funny and he walked funny.

He was about thirteen or fourteen years old and was wearing shorts and a tee shirt. Under the shorts and tee shirt his entire body was encased in a tight fitting, tan, cotton, body stocking. Here and there were patches of something seeping through.

I didn't know what it was and I didn't want to know. He was a terrible sight and I hoped my face didn't betray my feelings as I greeted them.

His mother told me the story. It seems he and some friends were trying to build a fire and they weren't having much success at it. Then he decided to help it along by pouring gasoline on it. There must have been some flame because that flame traveled up the stream and into the can. The can blew up and drenched him from the neck down in a sheet of burning fuel. He damn near died. His immediate future would consist of months and months of horribly painful skin grafts. His mother promised him flying lessons as an inducement to face that pain.

I felt so sorry for that kid. I am sure everyone else felt as sorry for him as I did but young men sometimes find it hard to express sorrow. They nicknamed him "Toast." They didn't call him that to his face of course but still it was always, "Hey Ron, how you and Toast coming along?," or "I see you have another lesson with Toast this afternoon." I gave them hell for this but of course they ignored me.

Boys will be boys.

The lessons began. I'll never forget the first time we walked down the line to the glider, it took forever. There was no way I was going to ask him to help me move the glider, he could not have done it. Just loading him into the cockpit and strapping him in must have brought him great pain. I could see it in his face. I had an aversion to even touching him but I had to.

At first the lessons went well. Most young students are rather ham handed with the controls and have a tendency to over control. He flew with a velvet touch, he had to, any thing else would hurt. That was fine in the beginning but I knew that soon he would be required to make full and rapid control inputs for some of the maneuvers and I wondered about that.

I don't think his mother realized just what all was involved.

I was stuck between a rock and a hard place and I had to tell her. Then one day when I found myself alone with his mother we had a long talk. I watched them drive away that day knowing I would probably never see him again.

To this day I am haunted by my decision. Did I do the right thing? It seemed to be the right thing at the time. I did the best I could. I often think about that kid and wonder where he is today and what he is doing. If you are reading this, I am sorry.

WINTER FLIGHT

For the first time in my life I had a fully assembled aircraft sitting in a hanger ready to fly in the winter.

A cold hard little snow blew diagonally across the road like swiftly flowing water. The partly cloudy sky allowed shafts of pale sunlight to dapple the otherwise flat, gray/white, monotonous landscape.

I drove around behind the hanger and parked to one side of the hanger door. My tires had left two inch deep tracks in the snow. Once inside the meager light of the entry door revealed the "Moni" motor glider tied down with its wings and tail blocked level with stands. I undid the doors' down locks and took a strain on the chain hoist. With a snapping of ice along the bottom edge, the door groaned and began to lift. Thirty-four pulls and it was fully open.

The little green eye of the battery charger let me know it was doing its job. I removed the canopy cover and opened the canopy. Gas on, choke on, throttle cracked, main and master switch on and I pushed the start button. It cranked and cranked and cranked but no matter how much I fooled with the choke and throttle it would not start. I turned the switches off and I was not a happy camper.

Getting the heavy toolbox from the car, I removed the plug cover and the spark plug from the left cylinder. It was wet and so was the one on the other side. I gave both cylinders and plugs a shot of starting fluid, re-installed them as rapidly as possible, and hit the starter again. After a few loud pops the engine caught. The throttle was set at 2500 RPMs and locked, the canopy closed and I got out of the prop blast as fast as I could. The air temperature and wind speed made me feel naked.

After letting it run for about five minutes I went back in and opened the throttle full. About ten seconds of that was all I could stand. It was as though I had been stripped of all my clothes and hosed down with ice water.

The tail was untied, the ship pulled outside and I got aboard. The "Moni" is a tight fit even though I am rather small. With all those clothes on I felt as though I was stuffed in there. It wasn't an easy job to get the belts on, the radio plugged in and the headphones on but I managed to do it. The canopy was closed and I hit the starter, the engine came to life without any problems.

The two inches of snow caused me a little concern. It wasn't the main wheel I was worried about, it is large enough to handle the snow but I didn't know about those tiny wheels out on the wing tips. Would they allow me to gain enough speed to lift the wings level or would they drag in the snow the entire length of the runway?

Since I was taking off to the south I did not have to taxi to the far end of the runway to begin my take off run. I firewalled the throttle and was on my way. It took a little longer to reach sixty miles per hour because of the snow but I made it. A little back pressure on the stick and she lifted off.

Surprise! A few inches of snow had transformed the familiar landscape into something I had never seen before from the air. I couldn't believe how different everything looked. It was beautiful in a totally different way.

There seemed to be a bigger patch of sunlight up north about five miles away and since I had no particular plans I decided to go play in it. After awhile I decided to fly over the Lake Shabbona State Park just to see what I could see. The lake was frozen over and there were dozens of ice fishermen down there. I wondered if they were having as much fun staring at a hole in the ice as I was flying around over them? Spotting deer sure was a lot easier. Their brown coats stood out against the white background.

Almost two hours had gone by since I took off, my tank was getting low and it was time to head back to the field.

Entering the pattern at the airport I was a little apprehensive. This would be my first landing on snow. It was a piece of cake. I taxied back to the hanger, shut down and pulled the plane back into the hanger. It was tied down and the tank filled. The battery charger was plugged in and the canopy closed and its cover replaced. The hanger door was closed and locked and as I drove away from the airport I realized I had discovered a whole new world.

HIGH SCHOOL CLASS

They show up every spring just like the robins. A big yellow school bus brings about thirty high school students out to the flying field. They are an aviation class from one of Chicagoland's suburban high schools, and this is their field trip. They are here to learn about aviation first hand.

I get a big kick out of them. The class is mostly boys but there are usually a few girls too. They are all pretty excited and they're all hyped up and ready to go. Someone always brings along a couple of Frisbees and a football and soon these are flying back and forth.

The class instructor has to be a saint to put up with this bunch. I guess all teachers are. He is the one who sets the whole thing up. He helps load the kids in the glider, runs the towrope, hooks the glider up and keeps things more or less organized.

By about ten in the morning we are all sorted out and ready to start flying. As I load each student into the glider I offer a choice of what type of flight they want, a "Mister Smoothy" or a "Whoop-de-do"? Then I explain that a "Mister Smoothy" is nice and gentle and will last longer than a "Whoop-de-do" which is more like a roller coaster but is shorter.

About 85% opt for the "Whoop-de-do. Once again I am surprised as to who chooses what. The quiet little gal wants the "Whoop-de-do" and the big boisterous jock wants a "Mister Smoothy." You just can't tell a book by its cover.

They've brought tons of food and by noon the barbecue grill is putting out a lot of smoke. These kids can really eat and that presents sort of a problem in the afternoon. You have to be very careful about giving a "Whoop-de –do" to anyone. One young man who apparently had a brat, two hot dogs and a hamburger for lunch, deposited them in small chunks all over the inside of my glider. I thought for sure the kid was cool but he surprised me. There wasn't any warning, he just sort of blew up.

By late afternoon the last student gets a ride, the food is all gone and the bill has been paid, by the class instructor. They all pile back into the bus and start the long ride home.

They'll be back, maybe not the same ones, but some just like them. It's a sign of spring, just like the robins.

THE LAST HURRAH

He told me that the reason he chose me to be his instructor was because I had gray hair. It is surprising how often an older student will do that. I guess they feel a certain kinship or connection with someone more their own age. It's true he was older than I was, but not all that much older.

One of his other hobbies was bowling and apparently all his teammates told him he was crazy to be taking up flying at his age. "Ron," he said, "this is my last hurrah, I really want to show those guys they are wrong." I assured him that I saw no reason why he couldn't learn to fly. God, how wrong I was!

He started off well enough but then things began to go to hell in a hand basket. One of his problems was that he never could keep track of where he put the airport. That is sort of important in any aircraft but even more important in a glider. There is a saying: "Takeoffs are optional, but landings are mandatory."

We would get off tow at the standard two thousand feet and after flying for a brief period, I would ask him where the airport was. He would become extremely nervous and move his head rapidly from side to side with his eyes bugged out, all the while expelling large amounts of breath. I told him to calm down and if he couldn't see the airport at first, to look for some landmark he could identify, get himself orientated and then he could look in the right direction for the airport. This didn't seem to help at all. He would just become so excited that on several occasions he looked directly at the airport and didn't even see it.

There were other problems too. He couldn't seem to grasp the concept that a glider can only go so far for a given altitude. On more than one occasion he got so far away from the field that I began to squirm in the back seat. I would let him go as far as I could, all the while hoping he would make that turn towards the airport and put me out of my misery, it never happened, I would have to take the controls and make another save.

The number of flights grew and grew in his logbook and for each flight I got a new gray hair or one fell out. We just weren't making any progress. Then one day while we were practicing landing patterns, he damn near killed me twice. He would enter the pattern at the proper height and then pull the spoilers full on and forget them. I would sit back there giving all sorts of verbal hints as to how low we were but he just ignored them and went happily on his merry way. When I couldn't stand it anymore I would take the controls and complete the landing.

The last two that day, were really bad. After I took over the controls I had to make a decision on the base leg of the pattern as to whether I should fly over the telephone wires or go under them.

One of the guys at the field caught the whole ugly thing on video. All you could see of the glider was its rudder slicing through the tall corn. If I could somehow dub in the sound track from the movie "Jaws" it would have been perfect. Then there is the shot of the glider bursting through the last row of corn, festooned with leaves on the wings leading edge and struts. It rolled to a stop about twenty feet in from the end of the runway. A voice off camera says, "Damn, that was low!" The cameraman says, "Naw, you should have seen the first one."

Up until that point I had kept my cool but then I blew it. I committed the cardinal sin for a flight instructor, I lost my temper. I accused the student of having fits of "intermittent brain death." He didn't say much, but the next Thursday, he always flew with me on Thursday, he had signed up with a younger instructor named Brad.

I thought this might be a good thing. Brad was younger and a good instructor. I was pretty frazzled. Perhaps Brad could do something with him. He certainly wasn't worth dying for anyway.

Thursday after Thursday went by and after the student left I would ask Brad, "Well, how did it go?" Brad would just smile and say, "Same o, same o." I felt sorry for Brad, hell, I felt sorry for the student.

Then one Thursday I noticed he was down on the schedule to fly with me again. We had a long talk and I told him that there was no one at the field that wanted to see him get his ticket more than I did. I told him we would try again.

So the pages in his logbook began to fill up. Flight after flight after flight was made with little or no progress. I was becoming frustrated with this guy, I couldn't figure out what to do with him anymore. He just wasn't going to make it and I really didn't want to tell him so. I couldn't just suggest that perhaps he should take up golf.

I had a talk with Todd, the young man who was managing the place that year. Todd suggested that the student take a *student evaluation flight*, with him and if he didn't measure up, he would tell him so. I thought that this was the best way to go, so I agreed with the plan. Perhaps I was just too close to the forest to see the trees.

After another Thursday of three rather harrowing flights, I told him I wanted him to take a check ride with Todd. He wasn't too happy with this suggestion and asked me to fly with him one more Thursday before he flew with Todd. I agreed to go along with this although I felt sure of the outcome.

On the very first flight that next Thursday, after we go off tow at two thousand feet, I asked that fatal question, "Where is the airport?" "Right over there," he said, pointing at it. I was elated. We flew around awhile and just as I began to squirm in the back seat he made a turn for the field, I was ecstatic. He entered the pattern at the proper altitude, he kept the air speed nailed, his turns were well coordinated, he touched down like a feather and we rolled to a stop.

We sat there awhile and then I asked him, "What was the one thing that was wrong with that landing?" He suggested that perhaps he should have used a little more spoilers on final. I told him that wasn't it and he said he couldn't think of anything else. I told him, "You just landed the wrong way on the active runway. You just landed into departing traffic." It wasn't a big deal that day; there wasn't any other traffic, but what if there had been? What if the Beech D-18 with a load of jumpers had been thundering down the runway? What if he had been solo?

There was a very long silence and then he opened the canopy and got out. "I see what you are trying to tell me," he said. Then he left and I never saw him again.

APPARITION

Sometimes things happen that you can hardly believe and if enough time goes by, you begin to wonder if they ever really happened at all.

It was a lousy day, real lousy. We wouldn't be doing any flying that day. The rain drummed loud and steady on the tin roof of the trailer and a cool damp wind blew in from the door. We were sitting around the table reading and doing some hanger flying, as usual. The coffee was good and I had my pipe going.

Then we heard it, even above the din of the rain we heard it, the unmistakable sound of two large radial engines slightly out of synch. We ran out on the porch to have a look, not really believing anyone would be flying on a day like this. Talk about scud running, this was ridiculous. Out of the gloom she came, in low from the east, I mean low. It went thundering down the field at no more than fifty feet. She looked like a specter out of the past, a real "Flying Dutchman."

It was all gray, a dull auto body primer sort of gray. I couldn't see any trim color or any markings on her. Every panel of her aluminum skin seemed to be dented, scratched, or stained. There were patches here and there and even though they were painted a gray, they didn't even come close to matching. Her engines were coughing up oil and it streamed in dirty black streaks from her cowls back to the trailing edges of her dented wings.

It was probably the most ratty looking "Beech D-18" I had ever seen. No one had wasted any TLC on that poor old gal. She dipped a wing as she went by and I swear I couldn't see anyone in her cockpit. Maybe it was just the fog, and the light, and the rain, but I couldn't see anyone. I felt a slight shiver go up my spine and it surprised me. Why did that happen I wondered?

Then she was gone. The gloom swallowed her up once again and the sound of her engines slowly faded away. Back into the fog and mist from where she came. The din of the rain returned and it was as though it had never happened. That one pass, that was all there was. We never saw her again.

If we had been in Florida or perhaps somewhere near the Mexican boarder I would have thought drugs, but this was Illinois. Why was she up on a day like this? Where did she come from? Where was she going? Who was she? Why?

SHIT HAPPENS

As a pilot, have you ever contemplated which control function you could lose and still survive the flight? Would it be the ability to control pitch, roll or yaw that you think you could live without, or should I say, continue living without? I once heard of a pilot who took off with the control column lock in place, thereby eliminating both pitch and roll control. That didn't pan out so well.

I suppose it would depend on which ship you were flying at the time. Some power planes seem to fly quite well with your feet flat on the floor. It seems the rudder pedals are there just to steer the thing around on the ground. So maybe you could get by without the rudder. On the other hand, there are at least two ultralights that I know of that don't have any ailerons, just lots of dihedral, and they fly quite well. So maybe you don't really need ailerons. In either case, crosswinds do present a bit of a problem.

There once was a student that completed a glider flight. When the ship came to a stop, I noticed that one of the ailerons was hanging straight down. It seems that a bolt in the control linkage had fallen out. He said he didn't notice any difference in the way the ship flew.

I am in the habit of giving the ship a good pre-flight before I fly it. I don't just kick the tire and light the fire. I know glider pilots who refuse to speak to anyone when they are giving their aircraft a pre-flight, maybe this isn't such a bad idea.

On one particular occasion, I really screwed up. Apparently something had distracted me. After doing what I thought was a thorough pre-flight on my "Moni" motor glider, I started the engine and taxied down to the end of the runway. I went through my pre-takeoff checklist and everything was normal including full control movement. I saw the aileron go up and down as it was supposed to. I took off and everything seemed normal. I flew around for awhile and then headed for Lake Shabbona, thirteen miles away. It was while circling the lake that I glanced out at my right wing and was surprised to see a bright shinny object at the end of the aileron. It was the aileron lock. How could I be that X!*$#% stupid, I thought. I couldn't believe the ship was flying. I could not notice any difference in turn performance and if anything, the "Moni" is an aileron type of ship.

Very carefully I flew back to the field and landed. I didn't want to shut down and get out of the plane to take the damn thing off, so I taxied up to a pilot who was disassembling his glider and motioned for him to come over. I raised the canopy and pointing out to the wing, asked him if he would be so kind as to remove the aileron lock. He looked at me as though I were crazy, walked out to the end of the wing and removed the lock, all the while shaking his head and muttering something to himself.

I took off and flew around for about an hour. When I landed I found the pilot who had been so helpful and offered him ten dollars if he wouldn't tell anyone what had happened. He said I was too late and that he had already told six people. I'll bet he did. I would have told more than that.

About a week later I was reading a model airplane magazine when I happened upon an article about model glider pilots experiencing high-speed aileron flutter on their gliders. Their ailerons were long and thin (strip ailerons) and were driven by their servos at the inboard end only. This was exactly the setup I had on my "Moni" motor glider. The solution to the problem was to immobilize the outboard ends of the ailerons. Their ailerons were just twisting and with the outboard ends fixed, they eliminated the problem of flutter without any noticeable loss of turn performance.

Now I wonder what would happen if I flew with both locks in place? I just don't have the guts to find out and I don't have the heart to ask anyone else to. I don't suppose I could find anyone who would do it anyhow. From now on, when I check control movement, I check both wings.

MY FAVORITES

I haven't flown all that many different aircraft but I do have my favorites. It probably doesn't matter if a pilot has only flown two different airplanes; he will still have his favorite. They are all different though, that's for sure.

Schweizer 2-33A

The Schweizer 2-33A is a great trainer as far as I am concerned. It will take lots of abuse at the hands of a student and it keeps right on flying. It is a very forgiving ship, too forgiving some people say. Well, maybe. I got to admit though; it does fly like a dump truck. You can trash the stick around like you are killing snakes and it just takes it's own sweet time. Sometimes I catch myself laughing at it.

Schweizer 1-26E

The Schweizer 1-26E is really a fun ship to fly. If the 2-33A is a dump truck, then the 1-26E is a sports car. It isn't all that high performance, but it will turn on a dime and give you nine cents change. It has the feeling of lightness and agility. I get a kick out of it.

Schleigher Ka-8B

The Schleicher Ka-8B is a ship I only flew one time for a little over an hour. I was so impressed with it I found myself looking at the want ads in the back of gliding magazines. It is an old German design and of modest performance but the thing seemed to fit me like a glove. I'll never forget how her controls felt, how she responded to the slightest input, I fell in love.

Blanik L-13

Of all the two place gliders I have flown, and there aren't that many, the Blanik L-13 has to be my favorite. I say that with mixed emotions. She is somewhat lacking in creature comforts but I love the way she flies.

The instructor sits in the back seat on cushions that seemed to be filled with old concrete. You sit way back in, more or less under the wing, bolt upright with your legs straight out in front of you. A stick the size of a small telephone pole juts up between your legs. The sides of the cockpit are high and the canopy is low. On a hot summer day the place is an oven.

One day I gave a ride to a guy who must have been about six foot four and he was wearing the biggest "Afro" I had ever seen. When I closed the forward canopy on him, his hair seemed to fill it. I got in behind him and I couldn't see anything but hair. I flew the entire flight looking out of the side of the canopy. Now I know how Charles Lindberg felt when he flew the Atlantic. I should have logged the flight as instrument time.

Despite all this I love the way this ship flies. It's as though the thing were on rails. It is big and heavy but yet it is responsive in it's own sort of way. It seems to evoke a feeling of confidence. You can crank her big old fowler flaps out and crawl around in a thermal at unbelievably slow speeds.

Mitchell B-10

As far as power planes go I guess my favorite has to be the Mitchell B-10. I know it isn't much of a power plane but I love it. It has bicycle wheels for landing gear, is covered with dress liner material, and has a go-cart engine for power but of all the things I have flown, I think I like it the best. Sitting out in the breeze, flying along at 35 MPH at 300 feet with the bugs glancing off your helmet is an absolute blast. The next homebuilt I constructed was the Moni, which is a totally different thing. I like the way it flies and what it can do, but I am fully enclosed under a canopy and I miss the bugs. It is hard to play you are the "Red Baron" when there isn't any wind in your face. So now I am building another ship which will get me outside again. I think I will like it. It is called the "Firestar II" and it has two seats. My wife has already informed me she isn't going up in *that thing*. I even put her name on the wing and she still won't go.

Moni Motorglider

The Moni was the second home-built aircraft that I constructed. It is an all aluminum motor-glider with a 25 hp engine. It is rather small and mine weighs only 311 lb.

As a motor-glider it is not all that high performance but can be soared in moderate lift. What I like most about it is the ability to self launch any tine, any place. You don't need a tow plane or a tow pilot, and it is extremely economical to operate. It is light on the controls, very responsive, and a joy to fly.

At the present time I have over 800 hours on mine and have had many enjoyable hours of soaring. Mine cruses at 87-95 mph so it can go cross-country, but not too far with only 4 gallons of gas.

I know other pilots will have other favorites, but these are mine.

MIKE

A couple of years ago my wife and I decided to do the fall color tour of the Smoky Mountains. Like any good "Propellerhead" would do, I immediately consulted my "Soaring Sites Directory" to see if any of them were located within a couple of hundred miles of our intended course. There were a few.

One Sunday morning we found ourselves at a place called "Chilhowee Gliderport," in Benton, Tennessee. It was early, real early; they weren't even there yet. We decided to tour the area for awhile and returned a little later to find the place in full swing. I walked into the trailer/office, just like the one we have at Hinckley Soaring and was greeted by a big friendly guy by the name of "Mike," who was the manager of the place. We chatted awhile and I told him I was an instructor at Hinckley and thought I would do a little soaring if that was possible. He looked at my logbook and we talked some more. Then he excused himself to take care of some other business.

I began to look at a big picture of the place taken from the air. For a "flatlander" like me from the cornfields of Illinois, this was something different. The damn place was nothing but trees and rocks. One had better not lose the airport around here.

I guess Mike must have seen the look on my face because he came over and asked me if I had a problem. I explained that I was a little apprehensive about the terrain and wasn't quite sure if I wanted to fly here or not. He told me to jump in the tow plane with him and he would give me a familiarization flight.

Five minutes later we landed and he asked me what I thought now. I told him I figured I could handle it. Then Mike said, "You see that guy standing over by that tree?" I said I did. "Well, he wants a demo ride, you take him up in the Grob 103." Not being one to turn down a free glider ride, I did.

Grob 103

The ridge wasn't working that day and there wasn't much thermal lift either but I decided to hang around and fly something anyhow. It seems to be the story no matter where I go to fly ridge. They always say, "Too bad, you should have been here yesterday." Oh well, one of these days I'll hit it right.

About three in the afternoon I decided to fly a ship I had never flown before, a Schleicher Ka-8B. I got the operations manual on the thing and studied it for awhile. I took a tow to two thousand feet and managed to stay up for a little over an hour. I really liked that ship and had fun flying it. It was a great day and I think of it often.

We hung around for a little while after I landed and then said goodbye to Mike. Just recently I heard that Mike is no longer with us. Too bad, he was a really nice guy. I only met him that one time but I will always remember him. Some guys are like that.

TRANSITION PILOTS

Not all the students I taught to fly gliders were rank beginners; some of them had a power license. These people are called "Transition Pilots" and they were adding a glider rating to their existing ticket.

All the power pilots I ever taught had certain traits in common. They always wanted to flare the glider when they landed. You don't flare a glider; you round out and land in a level attitude. They would not use enough rudder when they flew. Most of the power planes I ever flew could be flown with your feet flat on the floor most or the time. A glider has long wings, and when you push the stick one way to turn and don't use enough rudder, the nose will actually yaw the wrong way. It will eventually turn the right way but it is an uncoordinated turn and you could eat half a sandwich before it ever starts to turn.

I don't say any of this in a derogatory manner. When I took power lessons, I did not flare when I landed and I used too much rudder. My instructor thought I was trying to tear the nose wheel out of the old Cessna 150 and he would be screaming for me to "Get that yoke back in your guts and keep it there!" It is just that power planes should be flown one way and gliders another.

It impressed me how aware transition pilots are of other traffic. They would call out, "We have traffic at three o'clock." I would look and not see a thing, then I would look again and see a small speck in the sky about fifteen miles away. I would get a kick out of that.

Glider pilots are used to flying in much closer proximity. If one glider takes off and starts to circle in a thermal, you can bet the next glider will join him, and the next and the next. This is called a "Gaggle," and I have seen a half a dozen gliders all circling in the same thermal at the same time. The tightness of this situation sometimes amazes the transition pilot. I tell them that if you can look into the cockpit of the nearest glider and recognize the pilot, then things are cool. If, however, you notice that the pilot needs a shave, then you might want to add a little more distance.

Despite the differences between powered flight and gliding, I have never had a transition student who didn't tell me that glider training made them a better power pilot. Some of them fell in love with soaring and went out and bought themselves a glider.

MOLLY AND THE MONI

The first time I saw Molly, her mother brought her out to Hinckley Soaring and laid her on a blanket to play in the sunshine. I don't know how old she was but I would guess about two.

Maurice Chevalier sang a song in some movie that had a line that went, "Thank heavens for little girls, they grow up in the most delightful ways." Well that is what happened to Molly.

She must have been seventeen that day she walked down the field and saw my "Moni" motor-glider for the first time. I was very proud and I expected her to say something like, "Wow Ron, What a hot looking ship. You must be some pilot to fly that thing!" That isn't exactly what she said. "Oh," she squealed, "it's sooo cute. It looks like something that should be hanging from my brothers' bedroom ceiling. It looks like it came out of a toy store." I was very disappointed. That was the trouble with that ship. It was so small it didn't get any respect.

A few weeks later I had the Moni tied down and was sitting in a lawn chair by it, when a little girl and her father came walking by. The kid said, "Look daddy, a toy airplane, can I stand on the wing and you take my picture?"

At that time I was hauling the ship out to the field in it's trailer and assembling it. If the weather was predicted to be nice for a few days I would leave it assembled and tied down on the field. Occasionally I would return to find the propeller in a different position than the one I had left it in. People just couldn't keep their hands off it. It just didn't get any respect.

I finally decided that before I found footprints on the wing one day. I had better rent a hanger to keep it in. It just didn't get any respect.

CLOUDS

Every pilot I have ever met is somewhat of an amateur meteorologist, especially if a glider pilot. It is the weather that powers a glider. It allows us to make a long flight or causes us to sit on the ground and wish that we were making a long flight.

When I lived in the city it was easy to look out the window and if I saw rain, I would assume it was raining everywhere in the city. My view was restricted by the house and trees on the other side of the street.

Now that I live out in the boonies all this has changed. Sometimes when there is a storm brewing, I will jump in my jeep and head out to the airport just to watch it. If I look north from the runway it is probably ten miles or more to the horizon. I can see about thirty-two miles of horizon in 180 degrees. There is an awful lot going on in that thirty-two miles. I now realize that storms are in cells and can be quite localized. From my view at the flying field I can see it rain in one town while the next town just a few miles away is in clear sunshine.

Spending so much time at the airport as an instructor gave me plenty of opportunity to watch clouds. I used to look at a cloud and think it was more or less stationary; an unchanging mass of white in a blue sky. That isn't the case at all. A cloud is born as a tiny white wisp and can grow and mature into a gigantic Cumulus or even a Cumulonimbus (storm cloud). Then if I watch long enough, I can see it die and decay. It seems to get so big and then it begins to fall into itself and finally disappear or become a Stratus cloud.

I have seen a lot of really bad storms while working out at the field. Sometimes they approach with such speed that we don't have time to tie the ships down. When this happens we jump into the gliders and fly them on the ground.

It is just like flying a simulator. The pilot has full control of glider and it responds to all control inputs while balancing on its single wheel. It just doesn't go anywhere. I could have logged considerable time doing this. It is great fun but you can't log it.

On a few occasions I have witnessed what looked like elephant trunks hanging down out of a cloud. After dangling there for a while they would retract back up into the cloud. I don't know if they would ever actually become tornadoes but it sure looked like the beginning of one to me. The sky usually has a green look to it when this happens and it always makes me feel funny and I don't mean "Ha Ha" funny.

One evening after supper I went out to the field to watch a building storm. It was a humdinger. The wind blew so hard it rocked the trailer from side to side, the rain drumming on the metal roof was deafening and the lightening was spectacular. In a few hours it seemed to be all over and so I headed for home and arrived there around 8:30 PM. On the nine o'clock news that night I was amazed to hear that a tornado had touched down in Hinckley that evening. I laughed and told my wife that I sure didn't see any tornado.

The next morning as I drove to the field I noticed that one of our training gliders was missing its vertical fin. There was a strange ball of twisted metal sitting in the middle of the runway that turned out to be what was left of a Cessna 180 jump plane. The twin engine Beech D-18 had been blown clear to the other side of the runway but appeared to be undamaged. About a mile to the north in the middle of a bean field there was a blue and white Cessna 150 sitting upright on its gear. It too appeared to be all right, until I looked at it through a pair of binoculars. I drove over to have a look at it later and it was totaled. It must have gone all that way end over end and landed upright. There wasn't anything on the ship that wasn't bent.

Apparently the tornado hit the west end of the field where the jump school was located because things were a mess down there, they really got hammered. That was only 2000 feet from the trailer. The trailer was buffeted so badly that all the canned pop in the refrigerator was tumbled. I'll bet that would have been one hell of a ride. It must have happened between the time I left the field and the time I watched the nine o'clock news. It sure didn't happen while I was there. In a way I am sorry I missed it. I'll bet if I had been there, my eyes would have been big as saucers.

FOUR BOX TOPS AND A DIME

"Mom, how far away is Battle Creek Michigan?" I must have driven her crazy. It was just two days ago that I sent the four cereal box tops and a dime to get the instructions, "How To Fly A Piper Cub." I must have checked the mailbox sixteen times a day. It seems everything I ever sent away for as a kid, came from Battle Creek, Michigan. My "Jack Armstrong Secret Decoder Ring" came from there and everything else did too.

It took me two whole weeks to eat four boxes of a certain cereal but I finally got the required box tops. After searching the neighborhood trash cans I came up with five pop bottles which I took to the grocery store and got a two cent refund for each, that gave me the much needed dime.

I don't know how long it really took to get the book but it seemed like forever. I was convinced that Battle Creek was somewhere on the other side of planet earth, somewhere near China. Then one day I got home from school and there was a package for me on the kitchen table. I ripped the paper covering off and there it was, "How To Fly A Piper Cub."

It was the dead of winter and the snow was pretty deep but that didn't matter, I had to start my flying lessons now.

About two miles outside of town on the east side there was a small airport with a couple of airplanes tied down. I called my trusty friend "Corky" and we made a plan. After dark, when no one was around, we would walk the two miles through the snow and bitter cold to the airport. Once we were there Corky would crawl into the back seat of a plane with the flashlight and the instruction book and I would get into the front seat.

The lesson would begin. Corky would read the instructions with the flashlight and I would move the controls as instructed. It wasn't easy, I could barely reach the stick and rudder pedals even sitting forward on the edge of the seat. I made takeoffs, climbs, turns right and left, glides and landings. The stick was moved this way and that, the right and left rudder pedals were pushed as instructed and the throttle was advanced or retarded. Then it was Corky's turn and we would switch places. After about two hours of this the windows had a thick coating of frost, it was impossible to see outside anymore and we were about frozen stiff. We would pry ourselves out of the plane and trudge the two miles home through the snow and cold.

It took about four or five nights of this practice before Corky and I were convinced we could fly an airplane. I thought the book was very good as far as it went but they left out one important piece of instruction. They didn't tell you how to start the engine. Thank God!

BOOMER

It really didn't look all that good. My buddy and I were sitting on the deck of the line shack at Hinckley Soaring and they were closed. We were just smoking cigars and shooting the breeze. Talking about things that happened in the past and the friends that have come and gone.

The sunshine was being filtered through a hazy sky and there was very little breeze. At about one o'clock I noticed tiny cumulus clouds starting to form in the haze and the bug bit. Time to fly!

My buddy took me home and we said so long. I jumped into my Jeep and headed for the other airport, the one where I keep the Moni hangared. I pulled the Moni out, did my pre-flight and checked the fuel. I had 12 pounds aboard and decided not to top off the tank to keep the ship light. I didn't need the additional 12 pounds of a full tank for what I wanted to do. If I couldn't find lift with a half tank, it was a bummer.

At 2:15 PM I was rolling down the runway. The air was really bumpy and it was knocking the heck out of me as I climbed working any lift I could find. At 3500 feet altitude, I figured I was in lift so I throttled back till the engine cooled and then shut down. As luck would have, it I lost the thermal. Although I found spotty patches here and there, I was soon at 2000' again where I fired up the engine, let it warm up, gave it full throttle and started to search again. It's just like fishing. This time I really hit a "boomer" and as I climbed through 3500'again, I shut down. This time I didn't stop climbing. It was one wild ride. I wasn't quite centered so the lift was stronger on one side of the turn than the other. The vario was pegging on the strong side and I would roll off some of the bank, haul back on the stick and zoom up till the Moni would shudder. Then I would release backpressure and wrap it up in a steep bank and go zipping around for some more. This may not be the most efficient way to thermal but it sure as hell is the most fun. Visible chunks of altitude were being added to the altimeter in two to three hundred feet a pop. It looked like the lift was averaging around five hundred feet per minute. The sky was definitely improving. It was getting bluer and bluer and more and more cumulus started appearing.

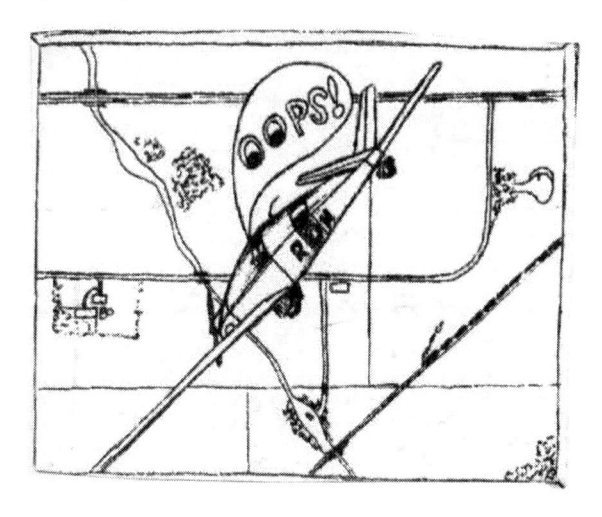

At one point in the flight something strange happened. It felt as though something pushed my tail straight up and for a moment I hung in the straps looking straight down at the farmlands. I recovered from the dive and although I was a little rattled, I decided I wanted to experience that again. For the second time I found myself looking straight down and this time I thought that perhaps I had a control problem.
After flying gingerly around for awhile I concluded there was nothing wrong with the controls. I had this problem once before with a student on a training flight in an SGS 2-33A. I now believe what happened was the updraft was so strong and sudden that it caused the relative wind to exceed the critical angle of attack and the wing simply stopped flying. My Moni will buffet at 47 mph and stall at 45 when eased into a stall from straight and level. There isn't a whole lot of time between 47 and 45 and this thermal was so violent and fast that I never felt the buffet, if there was one. My Moni only weighs 311 pounds and really gets knocked around in a lift.

Round and round we went, the Moni and I, the farms kept getting smaller and smaller. It topped out at 8200' and no matter how I tried I couldn't seen to get that additional 300' that would have given me an even 5000' gain. Some people are never satisfied. The additional 300 would have put me in the clouds anyhow and I really didn't want to go there. I probably would have but not for long.

Rolling level, I headed up wind and although I encountered more lift I didn't work it. I was getting cold and I'd had enough. Slowing up in the lift and speeding up in the sink but always flying straight we must have gone about six or seven miles and were down to 3000' when I headed back for the field. When I got near the pattern IP I was still at 2000'AGL so I circled until I was at 1000', flew the pattern and made a dead stick landing.

It was a personal best in the Moni for me and I was happy as a clam. The entire flight lasted one hour and sixteen minutes and I had an eighteen-minute fuel burn. That fuel burn included start up, warm up, back taxi and taxi back to the hanger after landing. What a day!

THE END

Every book must have an ending and I guess this is it. A lifetime of being a Propellerhead has been interesting to say the least. It has allowed me to do what I consider to be interesting things and in doing those things, I learned a lot that I never knew before.

They say that the best way to learn a subject is to try to teach it. As a flight instructor my students taught me something new every day. Of course, there were a few occasions when they taught me things I just as soon had never known.

Being a Propellerhead brought me in contact with a lot of very interesting people: students, passengers, instructors, pilots, builders; and others.

The farmer who's land I made a forced landing on, the old guy who gave me a lift to the airport, all of them were interesting and some of them I will never forget.

The things I have seen while flying could not have been seen in any other way. The way the land looks from up there in the early morning sunlight, the way it looks in the last rays of the setting sun, are forever etched in my mind. I have often wished that everyone in the world could have seen it that way.

I suppose I could have chosen any other hobby/sport and written a book about it, but I am glad I turned out to be a Propellerhead.

About the Author

Ron Martelet graduated from the Art Center College of Design in 1959 with a degree in Industrial Design. He went to work for Sears Roebuck and Company and retired after thirty years of service in 1989.

While at Sears he worked on over 100 different products. The variety of products to design is what kept him at Sears. The smallest of these products were Christmas tree light reflectors and the largest was a seventeen- foot, inboard/outboard cabin cruiser.

He holds several design patents, mostly for sewing machine designs. Ron never thought of his job as work and couldn't believe he could get paid for doing something that gave him so much pleasure.

His vocation was design but his avocation was aviation. His life long hobby is building model airplanes. One of his models is on display in the museum of the Academy of Model Aeronautics.

He also builds full size home-built (Experimental) aircraft and is presently flying two of them. The holder of both power-plane and glider ratings, he taught soaring for many years.

Ron also loves to ski, sail and write articles for aviation publications.